I0677587

beyond borders

Nepali literature in translation
Volume 1 | 2024

Translated by

JAYANT SHARMA

translateNEPAL
literature beyond borders

beyond
borders

Published by translateNepal, Sydney
nepaltranslate@gmail.com
www.translatenepal.com

Translation copyright © Jayant Sharma 2024
Edition copyright © translateNepal 2024

The moral rights of authors have been asserted.

A catalogue record for this
book is available from the
National Library of Australia

ISBN 978-1-7636836-0-0

All rights reserved. No part of this publication may be reproduced, stored in a retrieval system, or transmitted, in any form or by any means—electronic, mechanical, photocopying, recording or otherwise—without the prior written permission of the copyright owner.

FOREWORD

Through emotional expression, a transformative process began in the annals of the past, where certain entities evolved from mere animals into humans, with the pinnacle of this evolution manifesting in language. As language took shape, humanity embarked on a gradual ascent along the path of civilisation. In this journey, the emergence of pictorial writing, which initially reflected the conditions of the time, served as the precursor to the depiction of speech and eventually laid the foundation for script.

As the written word advanced, fuelled by the pursuit of education, the contours of literature began to take shape. This marked the birth of an extraordinary domain, where literature set its aims: to cultivate the essence of humanity, satisfy the thirst for knowledge, and inspire the creation of a more beautiful world by confronting and challenging the harsh realities of existence. It continues to evolve by deconstructing knowledge, science, philosophy, ethics, and human character. In this context, literature emerges as a guiding force in human life, teaching individuals what it truly means to be human and how to live authentically as such. It highlights the importance of discerning, selecting, and embracing or rejecting what is essential to human existence.

Humans initially roamed the Earth as savages and nomads, later adapting to life in caves and rudimentary shelters as civilisation advanced. With the discovery of agriculture, they began constructing huts, marking the transition to settled communities. However, this development was not uniform across the globe. Different groups evolved in different ways, leading to varied behaviours and languages that expressed their emotions. The linguistic diversity among these groups was vast, extending not merely into hundreds or thousands of languages but hundreds of thousands. Those who developed a script and passed it down to their descendants managed to preserve their languages and history over time. In contrast, those who relied solely on spoken language but lacked a written record faced a different fate—countless such languages were lost, and this process of extinction continues. With each language lost, not only did the language itself vanish, but the unique knowledge, science, and history it carried gradually faded as well.

In contemporary times, a significant endeavour has emerged: to internalise diverse emotions and channel one's own sentiments, with the aim of transforming the world into a shared space of human experience. This endeavour seeks to unite the emotions of individual homes into a collective sphere, and it is this convergence that embodies the expansion of emotional languages—namely, translation.

Translation serves as an extension of one's original art, culutre, literature, and philosophy. Through this process, emotions are granted the wings to soar beyond their origins. Translation becomes a divine artistic and intellectual tool, allowing individuals to travel the world while asserting their essence and originality. Today, the vital task of disseminating, nurturing, and preserving emotive expression is safeguarded through the very act of translation.

In the vast expanse of literary development over thousands of years, the evolution of Nepali language and literature has become notably significant only in the past two centuries. Yet, the pride we derive from this relatively recent literary tradition, which stands alongside the established literatures of millennia, is undeniable. This truth becomes evident when we examine both world literature and Nepali literature in tandem.

However, a pressing question arises: why have we been

unable to elevate and disseminate Nepali literature to the same level as other world languages? The answer is straightforward—because we access other literatures through translation, but when it comes to our own literature, the challenge lies not in understanding it ourselves, but in making it accessible and appealing to others. How do we foster interest in others to read and appreciate our literary heritage?

Indeed, the challenges we face stem from a lack of skilled translations, competent translators, and the necessary mechanisms to promote our literature on the global stage. Yet, it is through dreams that the seeds of thought are sown; these thoughts, in turn, propel us toward our destination, with each step serving as a launchpad for achieving our goals. As such, this marks the beginning of that journey—*Beyond Borders*.

In this initiative, diverse genres of Nepali literature—poetry, fiction, essays, and dramas—are represented, featuring both legendary figures from modern Nepali literature and contemporary literary voices. Their established, timeless works, now adorned with the beauty of translation, are poised to spread their wings and explore the world beyond our borders.

From the profound verses of the great poet Devkota's *Yātri* (Pilgrim) to Gopal Prasad Rimal's evocative *Ek Din Ek Choti Aunchha* (A day once in an era), and extending to the poignant reflections in Saraswati Pratikshya's *Chihaanma Phool* (Flowers on the grave), the ink of the pen dives deep into the human experience.

In the realm of short stories, it spans from the classic *Parālko Aago* (A blaze in the straw) by the fiction maestro Guru Prasad Mainali to the modern narrative of Bina Theeng Tamang's *Kāmred Anjana* (Comrade Anjana).

In drama, it includes the celebrated playwright Bhimnidhi

Tiwari's iconic play *Sāndé* (The Bull), as well as the contemporary work of Ashesh Malla, *Hāmi Basanta Khoji Rahechhau* (In quest of Spring).

In the field of essays, it ranges from the historical insights of Baburam Acharya in *Bhot, Madhesh, Ra Nepal* (Tibet, Madhesh, and Nepal) to the modern contemplations found in Roshan Sherchan's *Ma Kina Kavita Lekchhu* (Why I write poetry).

Thus, *Beyond Borders* aspires to uplift Nepali literature, contributing nourishment to its literary garden, albeit in modest quantities. It is important to recognise that, with continued effort, these contributions will gradually accumulate, like drops of water filling a vessel, sustaining and enriching the Nepali literary landscape in the long run.

Sudarshan Shrestha
Writer and filmmaker

POETRY

SHORT STORY

DRAMA

ESSAY

Poetry

PILGRIM

Laxmi Prasad Devkota

To which temple do you journey, O pilgrim?
Which holy ground beckons your steps?
What offerings shall you carry forth?
And how shall you present them?
Riding upon the shoulders of humanity,
To what divine abode do you aim?

Behold the majestic columns crafted from bone and sinew,
Flesh forms the temple walls,
With the mind as its gilded dome,
And the senses as its portals,
The coursing rivers within veins serve as sacred waters,
The human form, a temple complete.

To which sanctuary shall you tread, pilgrim?
Which door leads to the shrine?
For God reigns inside the chambers of the heart,
The radiant light of consciousness adorns the brow,
A grand temple in human form, stands in the worldly expanse.

Why seek distant pilgrimages when divinity dwells within?
How far shall you wander upon the surface,
When God abides in the depths?
To discover Him, ignite the luminous flame of your heart.

God walks alongside the weary traveller stranded on the road,
He kisses the hands of those who perform noble deeds,
With a magical touch, He blesses upon the mortal brows.

God's voice resonates in the birdsong by the wayside,
He sings in the symphony of human suffering and anguish,
Yet, His divine presence eludes mortal eyes and ears.

Wanderer, which temple do you go, to what unfamiliar land?
Return, dear pilgrim, and humbly serve the feet of humanity,
Heal their excruciating wounds with soothing balms,
For in every human face, let His divine countenance smile. ◆

A DAY ONCE IN AN ERA

Gopal Prasad Rimal

A day comes once in an era,
Bringing disarray, upheaval, and profound change.
The mute begin to speak, anguished lips find their voice.
Those thought suppressed, rise up for retribution.
Those believed departed, return again and again.
Those thought asleep, wake and walk up fervently.
Those deemed dead and discarded, rise vehemently.
All turn into glowing embers, a storm begins to rage.
Cowards become fearless, a wave of energy surges.
A turmoil breaks through, transgressions are unmasked.
A day comes once in an era. ◆

TEACHING MY DAUGHTER READ THE MAP

Bijaya Malla

Red blood draws the borders,
like terraces etched in fields
across the stretches of every nation.
Here lies India, and there, Pakistan—
the stark dividing line in between
drawn with the blood of Hindus and Muslims.
Here is Germany, there, England;
here, Russia, and there, Japan.
Witness Hiroshima and Nagasaki nearby,
consumed by atom bombs!
This is Europe in bare bone,
haunted by the specter of Hitler's terror.
This is America—
land of dollars,
creator of the atom bomb,
harbinger of peace.
Everywhere,
red blood carves the lines,
and humanity is trapped inside,

like pigeons in a cage.

My daughter,
(a day may come, someday)
when, united,
everyone
hand in hand,
embracing one another—
Negroes, Aryans, and Mongols,
Palestinians, Dravidians, and Blacks—
will pour out from the depths of their eyes,
washing these lines of blood away.

And then,
after a long time—
my daughter,
a day might come
when, no matter how much you search,
you will find no trace of the red line. ◆

WHAT A LIFE IS THIS LIFE!

Hari Bhakta Katuwal

Emptied from within,
yet masquerading survival on the surface.
Devoured by the dread of atoms,
Haunted by the phantom of woes.
What a life is this life!

Condemned to rest with heads cradled on gun muzzles,
Bound to live with footsteps dancing on razor's blade,
Shutting eyes is a perilous gambit,
and opening them, an even greater risk.
What a life is this life!

This life—
Resembles delicate glass bangles,
on display in the shop's window,
shattering ere they grace a maiden's wrists.
Like flimsy rubber sandals,
snapping unpredictably along the journey.
What a life is this life! ◆

MY SQUARE

Bhupi Sherchan

Within the narrow alleys lies my square,
What not you find here, everything and bare.
Countless diseases,
Endless hunger,
Relentless sorrow,
But happiness alone is absent—
One thing that is forbidden here.
Within the narrow alleys lies my square,
What not you find here, everything and bare.

In this very square of mine—
Gods made by humans,
And humans made by gods,
Both reside!
Yet, both are distressed,
Both are dejected.
Humans are distressed because
They're bitten by fleas all night,
And smitten by wealth all day.

And the gods are dejected because
People have stopped worshipping them,
Stopped showing reverence.

Hence, in this very square of mine—
Both gods and humans,
In a tumult of curses,
Clash foreheads in discontent.

Within the narrow alleys lies my square,
What not you find here, everything and bare. ◆

THE HEN MUST NOT CROW

Kunta Sharma

Always, always on the rooftops,
In the courtyards, over the balconies—
The rooster cranes his neck,
Shakes his comb,
Perched in his place of pride.
It is his right to crow,
To raise his voice.
But the hen? She must only cluck softly,
Swallowing her lumps of resentment in silence.
Her duty is to lay eggs,
To sit on the nest,
To hatch chicks,
And nurture them devotedly.
She must not laugh freely,
The hen must not crow.

She must speak cautiously,
Lacing her words with respect,
Bow down at their feet,

Wear the flower of servitude in her crest.
She must not step over the line,
Must not ask for rights.
She must not laugh freely,
The hen must not crow.

Tears are her weapon,
A smile, her shield.
She must wield them as the situation demands,
Use them as circumstances require.
She must not speak the truth,
Must not unveil the curtains of dark.
She must not laugh freely,
The hen must not crow.

She must not step forward,
Must not stand in the way.
"Master, Master," she must chant,
Work tirelessly like a machine.
She must not set foot in new places,
Must not entertain fresh ideas.
She must not laugh freely,
The hen must not crow.

But what if she dares to crow?
Great misfortune will befall,
Policies and rules will rage.
She will face a mountain of obstacles,
She may drown in rivers of tears.
Dreams may shatter,
Life may unravel.
The eggs in her nest

May rot without reason.
The tender life of chicks
May nip in the bud.
She may face assaults,
She may face annihilation.
So she must not awaken consciousness,
Must not draw back the veil of darkness.
She must not laugh freely,
The hen must not crow.

When buried awareness
Seeks to flow,
When it defies stagnation,
Taking bold strides,
When light stirs,
And brave hearts speak out,
When the truth is finally spoken,
Terrorising barbarities
May awaken all at once,
Striking the death knell against life,
Blowing the conch of an unyielding thought.
So without great courage,
Without firm support,
She must not enter the bush of thorns.
She must not laugh freely,
The hen must not crow. ◆

WHAT'S THERE IN THE MOUNTAINS!

Min Bahadur Bista

1. Sprung from the spring,
Darting here and there,
Pausing now and then,
Yet never once
Looking back—
Instead, fiercely kicking
At the sickly mountains,
Standing like statues on either side,
The river rushes on,
Leaving the land behind.

2. With a red scarf
Neatly tied around their bags,
And a rusted *khukuri*,
Unsharpened for ages,
Hung at their waist,
Young sons march forward,
Leaving behind their ailing parents
To tend to homes that feel like morgues.

They take with them their partners though,
Abandoning their birthplace.

3. Carried away by an untimely wind,
Blowing in from an unknown land,
Delicate buds of flowers,
Tender green leaves,
Fly aimlessly,
Stripping bare and ugly
The once majestic mountain ranges,
Where trees,
Like soldiers in parade,
Stand in sorrowful silence.

4. After a long drought,
Caught in relentless storms and downpours,
Flocks of pigeons,
Homeless like squatters,
With chests dried from drought
And bodies drenched by rain,
Wander aimlessly,
Knowing neither shelter nor sustenance,
Lost,
Sometimes drifting east,
Sometimes west.

5. There's nothing in the mountains
Worth writing a poem about—
Truly, nothing in these mountains
That any writer could pen an essay on.
Like soldiers
Returning home

After years in foreign soil,
Saying again and again,
"Damn, what's there in these mountains?"
Yes, there's nothing,
Absolutely nothing, in these damn mountains.
But wait, there is something—
Like mothers who have lost their newborns,
There are river sources,
Shedding tears of deep sorrow.
Though the rivers may leave,
There are still stagnant ponds,
Breeding filth and frogs,
Sitting unmoved, like rocks.
There are old couples,
Tending their homes, waiting for death.
There are mountains with faces worn out,
And trees arrested in their youth.
And a flock of squatter pigeons,
Bleeding tears from their eyes,
Coos with such pain
That it cuts to the heart. ◆

IN THE YARD OF REVOLT

Pradeep Gyawali

Throughout the night,
Wrapped in the cloak of constellations,
Children engage in a wrestling symphony,
Their backs turning to the courtyard's expanse.
Come morning,
A marathon unfolds, a race to fish for rice grains
In a pond awash with starch.
From the lashes of her eyes,
Kamini Bhauju[1], miscarried, lets fall the morning dew,
And from his quivering lips, songs unsung,
Presiding as a referee,
This is Lato Kāmi from our village.

Yellowing leaves of totalitarianism have fallen,
Green buds of democracy have burgeoned,
Yet he stands resolute,
Like the riverside pebbles
Or the withered guava tree in his yard.

---

[1] Kamini bhauju: A term used to address the wife of Lato Kāmi, the blacksmith.

Though the red sun pierces the dark clouds
In the eastern sky's ascent,
His kitchen garden mirrors the desert's kin.
Inside the barn, the barren heifer moans,
Yet, unmoving, he persists—
Provoking ancestral dogs to bark,
Pleading for alms door to door.
"Give a little more, 'tis the children's hunger!"
Upon the landlord's courtyard he stands,
Reciting mantras,
This is Lato Kāmi from our village.

Dreaming of grand terraces in a vast mansion,
He watches from a melancholy porch
As termites leisurely devour the rafters.

Let no one beckon him to toil today!
No time for labour,
For he smolders his own agony in the forge,
Hammering the iron of his anger on the anvil,
Trickling tears upon the bellows,
Dipping in the whetstone of sweat,
Sharpening the trowel of revolt—
This is Lato Kāmi from our village. ◆

THE BIRTH OF PRIDE

Sudarshan Shrestha

In the dearth of pride,
The chains of fervour break free,
Proclamations in times both right and wrong
Sprinkle death across the atmosphere.
On a stage where corpses twitch,
The hypocritical heart lays its traps.
When scarecrows claim the throne,
Even flowers of fire
Turn to ashes on the deathbed.
The muddy visions of the present
Succumb to false conspiracies of upheaval.
With each spewed word,
The rule morphs with a cunning change.

Pride perishes as you writhe in thirst,
Yet at that moment, determination is born.
How long will swords be wielded against truth?
With determination over truth,
Pride is reborn. ◆

BHIMSEN THAPA'S SUICIDE NOTE

Momila

Unaddressed remnants of all remaining addresses:

In the annals of history,
On a day of untimely storms and rain,
In a distant village exiled within its own borders,
From the old portrait of the patriot Amar Singh[1],
Proudly hung upon the wall—
The eyes suddenly fell.
Perhaps from that very moment,
The visionaries of this nation
Lost their sight.

Soon, the ears slipped down.
Since that day, the rulers of this land
Must have turned deaf.

Gradually, the nose and mouth followed.
From that instant, atop a reeking mountain of corpses,

[1] Amar Singh Thapa was a prominent Nepali military leader and statesman who played a crucial role in defending Nepal against British forces during the Anglo-Nepalese War.

The dissonant anthem of nationalism
Must have echoed through this desolate land.

Piece by piece, from the portrait—
The hands fell,
The feet fell.
Since then, noble hands
Must have been forced to commit suicide.
Since then, before a step could be taken,
The destiny of this nation
Must have gone astray.

At last, when only the skeleton remained,
From the portrait of Amar Singh,
The brain and heart too fell.
Perhaps from that moment,
The rulers of this land
Became nothing more than statues—
Adorned with colours and garlands,
Yet void of consciousness and compassion.

To lift such a collosal curse,
Bhimsen Thapas[2] must become corpses, not statues!

— Yours truly,
Bhimsen Thapa

"Just now, you were listening
To Bhimsen Thapa's suicide note.
And before wrapping up:

---

[2] Bhimsen Thapa was a notable Prime Minister of Nepal who played a key role in the consolidation of the Gorkha Kingdom but was imprisoned and killed in 1839 as a result of political intrigue and accusations of treason.

Today's headlines—
The nation is stunned by the patriot Bhimsen Thapa's suicide.
After Thapa's death, when his clenched fist was opened,
The random fortune lines on his palm,
The map of this land, and
The skeletal remains of Amar Singh in the hanging portrait
Are reported to be exactly the same." ◆

RUMOUR IN THE FISHERMEN'S VILLAGE

Shrawan Mukarung

As the rumour
Of stars drowning in the river
Rapidly spread through the village,
He rose early in the morning
And made his way to the river with his fish-hook.

Among the stars,
He was particularly fond of Polaris.
The reason being—
The Pole Star peeked in through his backdoor
And spilled all over his bed,
Whether he slept on an empty stomach at night
Or in a drunken stupor.
The Polaris
Gently sat on his forehead,
And he shone brightly.

With focus,
He set traps upon the bosom of the river.

From a distance,
A group of children pranced about—
"Hello, fisherman uncle!
We've found the droppings of a star."
They touched and examined it one by one
And reached a conclusion,
Their voices harmonising—
"The star's droppings look like stones."
He continued to set traps,
But the star never got ensnared.
Instead, plenty of fish got caught
And served as snacks for the entire village.

Now,
He was more determined to catch the Polaris.
So he set traps
Even while ferrying passengers across the river in a boat.
The children lifted the shores with their shouts—
"Hey, fisherman uncle!
Please catch the star quickly for us."

It was monsoon time,
One night,
A massive flood surged in,
And while engrossed in fishing the Pole Star,
The heartless flood
Swept him away.
The next day,
In the early hours of the morning,
Another rumour circulated in the village—
"A beautiful moon also drowned in the river." ◆

THE SCHOOL OF REVOLUTION

Avaya Shrestha

After meeting that melancholic girl,
I suddenly realised—
The system, like a glossy cover on a cheap book,
Is but a grand cesspool.

Love and compassion, in this country,
Like a pair of *Dalit* lovebirds martyred,
Drift apart in the raging floods of Bheri.
Justice, like the corpse of Dharmabhakta[1],
Hangs on the slender *Khari* tree,
With flowers of meagre joy blooming slowly around it.
Cruelty, like a fugitive convict,
Runs rampant on the street, wielding a sword.

Like the hollow smile of a chronic patient,
Change, in this country, is merely
A sheeny chestnut seed
Riddled with mold within.

---

[1] One of the four martyrs of Nepal who fought against the autocratic Rana regime; he was arrested and hanged in Sifal, Kathmandu.

After meeting that dejected girl,
I suddenly felt—
Prostitution, like the rebellion's fury,
Is a formidable resistance.

Like a deceased poem buried beneath the weight of words,
Peace is but a grand cemetery, adorned lavishly.

Humanity is that shrill scream of the nun
Raped in the backstreet of the monastery.

Like the unrequited love of Shurpanakha[2],
Your valour is but a guinea pig.

What is the connection between
this endless, heart-shattering pain
and truth, as fleeting as nature?

After meeting that melancholic girl,
I realised—
She, as invincible as an ever-flowing river,
Is the first school forgotten by the revolution. ◆

---

[2] A demoness and sister of the demon king Ravana in the Hindu epic Ramayana; her
nose was cut by Lakshmana as punishment for her attempt to seduce him.

THE WIND'S LANGUAGE

Sarita Tiwari

Even the wind speaks its own language.

Like a carefree lover,
it whispers songs of love
into the ears of leaves,
then darts off, sending tickles
through their bodies.

Fiercely shaking the branches,
it wages a gentle resistance
against the directions
and walks away on the path it discerns.

It whirls the sands by the riverside
into ferocious quicksand of dust,
gathering foliage and bronze flowers,
then sprints away, sweeping off—
the speed of light!
the motion of the Earth!!

In this world,
the most silent thing you imagined,
even the wind's lips hold
the most powerful language.

When the quiet conscience
within this three-pound brain,
in the last moment,
refuses to think or speak,
when it loses the capacity to express,
the wind will gently push it forward,
carrying me to the other side of the Earth.

I have human lips,
I bear the pain of history,
I carry wounds with dried bloodstains.

In this ocean of silence,
not speaking up is also a strong violence.
I will learn the art of voice
with the wind's lips
and return.

O, dare you listen! ◆

FLOWERS ON THE GRAVE

Saraswati Pratikshya

No matter how much was planted,
The flowers never bloomed—never bloomed on the grave!

In the midst of singing,
The verses of the song began to weep on their own,
In the midst of laughter,
The corners of the lips started to cry on their own,
Along the height of this lament,
The *sarangi*[1] strings drifted,
Into the floods of desolate nights,
Those waiting for the light were swept away,
Thousands of voices drowned in chorus,
At the margins of this ugly current.
No matter how much was planted,
The flowers never bloomed—never bloomed on the grave!

With monotonous, hollow sighs
Of false emotions,

---

[1] A 4-stringed traditional Nepali folk instrument, similar to a fiddle.

Some
Turned graves into begging bowls,
Some
Made graves a ladder to climb higher.
Alas!
Right beside the graveyard,
Carrying skeletons in mind and body,
The ancient poor of society still stare at the graves,
And still remains the same,
The ancient tale of flowers that never bloomed on the grave!

For those who bled for the country,
Where is the value of their blood?
When scarecrows ride the palanquin of sacrifice
To the palace of power,
How can flowers bloom
On the graves of martyrs,
Where they should have actually flourished?

No matter how much was planted,
The flowers never bloomed—never bloomed on the grave! ◆

short story

A BLAZE IN THE STRAW

Guru Prasad Mainali

Gauñthali, Chamé's wife, had a remarkably cutting way of speaking. Despite his attempts to be courteous, she consistently skewed the conversation and introduced topics that would lead to arguments. As a result, the couple found themselves quarrelling every few days.

One evening, upon returning home from a day of ploughing, Chamé discovered that Gauñthali had locked the house and gone to the village to attend a wedding. Exhausted and hungry after his long day's work, Chamé began stowing away the yoke and plough and tethering the bull. Just then, Gauñthali arrived, walking down the hill. At the sight of her, Chamé's anger surged—there wasn't even a fire lit, let alone a meal prepared! Gauñthali hurried to unlock the door and rushed off to fetch water, while Chamé kindled a fire in the hearth and proceeded to fill his pipe with tobacco.

He sat perched on the doorstep, smoke billowing from his pipe like an impending storm cloud. Gauñthali returned, carrying a waterpot on her hip. Just as she was about to step inside the house, Chamé yelled, "This bitch has spent the whole day flirting with other men and still has the audacity to act naive!"

With that, he lashed out, kicking her hard. Gauñthali staggered and collapsed at the doorway, shattering the waterpot into pieces and splattering water across the threshold. As Gauñthali prepared to gather the broken shards and toss them into the yard, Chamé's voice boomed again "Don't stay another moment in my house! Leave and find your way elsewhere!" He grabbed her by the pigtail and dragged her out, hurling her into the yard.

Gauñthali had acknowledged a portion of the blame and remained silent even as he kicked her. However, when he grabbed her by the hair and dragged her out, she could no longer contain her emotions. She snapped, "Take your filthy hands off me! My poor parents, blinded by their ignorance, handed me over to a butcher! I'd rather drown than live as the wife of a pauper!"

"This bitch thinks her father's a rich man! Were it not for him slaving away in the fields for the whole village, he'd struggle to put food on the table! And yet, she brags about her parents!" Chamé barked, delivering another kick.

Gauñthali let out a piercing cry at the top of her voice. A group of village children had gathered on the terrace ridge, drawn by the spectacle unfolding before them. "Hey, you little lumps of clay, what's so exciting that you've come to watch?" Chamé shouted, picking up a stick to chase them away. The children scattered up the hill, their laughter resonating in the air.

Tears streamed down Gauñthali's face, yet Chamé nonchalantly unfurled a woven rush mat and settled down to sleep on the veranda.

II

The following morning, Chamé took out the plough-bull and headed to the paddy field with an empty stomach. When he returned home in the evening, he found Gauñthali gone. The neighbours informed him she had packed her bags and left for her parents' house.

The buffalo remained in the yard, and upon seeing Chamé, let out a loud bellow. Chamé gave it fodder and released the calf before grabbing a pail to start milking. At first, the buffalo gave a few streams of milk, but then, without warning, it kicked Chamé hard and darted away. The force of the kick sent him flying into a pile of dung, while the pail clattered three yards away. His loincloth and waistcoat were smeared with dung.

Spotting a sturdy stick leaning against the wall, Chamé grabbed it and swung a couple of times, but the the buffalo snapped its tether and bolted into Kokalé's maize field. Chamé tried to lure it back, but the animal kept leaping side to side in a state of panic. In moments, the freshly cultivated maize field transformed into a trampled expanse of straw.

From the edge of the yard, Kokalé's mother hurled a curse at Chamé, "You lout! May your fertility fade away! May cholera have the last of you! Just yesterday, you thrashed your wife, and today you're abusing the buffalo, destroying someone else's entire year of hard work! As if you're the only one with a temper! Maybe the moron thinks he's tough! Just last year, Dhanbiré knocked you out with a single punch, and there you lay bedridden all monsoon, and yet you still think you're strong! Why don't you show your bravery to a stranger instead of taking it out on your wife and a helpless animal? Come evening, you're up to something, stirring up trouble and throwing the whole village into chaos!"

A wedding celebration was in full swing at Dhanbiré's house. The village younkers were thoroughly intoxicated, their spirits high from the alcohol. Kokalé, dressed in women's clothes and posing as a *maruni*[1], was energetically beating a *madal*[2] and dancing, while the rest of the revellers clapped in rhythm and sang along, adding to the festivity.

Suddenly, Kokalé's sister arrived, bringing news of the damage to his maize field. Kokalé quickly dashed toward the field, still wearing his *maruni* skirt. The sight of his unusual attire seemed to excite the buffalo further—it raised its tail and pranced even more wildly. The few remaining ears of maize were on the brink of being crushed.

Seeing the destruction of his crops, Kokalé's anger flared. He stormed over and, in frustration, slapped Chamé twice across the face. Poor Chamé, miserable and defeated, stayed silent. It took the effort of four or five men working through half the night to finally drive the buffalo away.

III

The next morning, as Chamé made his way back from the spring with a waterpot balanced on his shoulder, he ran into Juthé Damai's wife descending the hill. Chamé shared a close friendship with Juthé, and affectionately referred to his wife as 'sister-in-law.'

Seeing him carrying the water, she remarked, "Oh, it's strange to see a man fetching water!"

"Well, Sister-in-law, what choice do I have? I sent the bitch back to her parents. If I don't fetch water, who will?"

"But if you beat her senseless, did she really have any choice?"

---

[1] A traditional Nepali folk dance performed by women during festivals.
[2] A traditional Nepali hand drum used in folk music.

"Her tongue cuts like a blade. What else could I do but put her in her place?"

"Maybe her tongue's become that sharp because of your beatings."

"Oh, hush! I haven't forgotten how thoroughly Juthé thrashed you last Dashain! Did you dare to speak up then?"

"Ha! A single beating, you say? He might seem caring now, but there was a time when not a day passed without a beating. Evenings, after his drunken escapades in Bhoté Gauñ, he'd find any excuse to pummel me. Festival occasions were even worse. After a few rainy days, my body still aches from those beatings! Yet, even after all these years, I don't think I've ever spoken back to him."

"Yes, indeed! So why do you say that my beatings made her cheeky? If she had been as modest as you, I would have treated her like a deity!"

"Anyway, there's no point in arguing with a foolish woman. How much longer will you keep fetching your own water? Tomorrow, go and bring her back."

"If she comes to her senses, the door is open for her return. But I'd rather be an outcast than go and get her back!"

Chamé was draped in a waistcoat over a half-sleeved shirt, with a loincloth tied lopsidedly around his waist. His black cap, stained with dirt, rested on his head, and a vermilion tika marked the space between his eyebrows. With a waterpot slung over his shoulder and a thin line of moustache set against his dark complexion, Chamé carried a style all his own.

IV

One morning, Chamé lounged on his veranda, leisurely puffing on a bamboo hookah. Down the hill, Juthé Damai descended. Leading the way was Juthé, holding his son, while his wife trailed behind, clutching a small bundle of clothes under her arm. As soon as he spotted Chamé, Juthé burst into laughter and called out cheerfully.

"How's everything going, brother?"

"Oh, not too bad, my brother!"

"Since you've chased your wife away, now sit back and enjoy the moment!"

Juthé and his wife shared a deep, affectionate bond. Whenever Juthé headed to the Majhi village for his tailoring work, he always took his wife along. During their journeys, they'd discuss the ups and downs of their household, both on their way to the village and back. In the evenings, as Juthé placed the lamp on its shelf, he would recite verses from the *Virata Parva*[3], and his wife, while washing the pots, would listen attentively. Should Juthé ever fall ill, his wife would diligently seek out the village's shamans and healers. Occasionally, on his way to fulfil tailoring duties for the Bishtas—the landlords— Juthé would engage in playful banter with his wife or comically crane his neck and roll his eyes at other passers-by. His wife would chuckle and tease, "You might be growing older, but your sense of humour is as sharp as ever!"

Juthé was also deeply devoted to his religious practices. At the break of dawn, he would commence his day by bathing in the spring. Following this ritual, he would anoint himself with sacred ashes from the spot where the women boiled their clothes. Engaging in this serene moment, he would recite a hymn something like, "Assuming a semblance akin to lightning, the Lord soared to the heavens in an instant."

As Chamé reflected on Juthé's harmonious domestic life, a wave of sorrow washed over him. At Juthé's home, they would

---

[3] The fourth book of the Hindu epic Mahabharata, detailing the Pandavas' 13th year of exile spent in disguise at the court of King Virata.

have likely finished their dinner and begun reading from the *Virata Parva*, while at his own home, discord and clamour would be on the rise. Juthé and his wife shared a deep affection, enjoying leisurely strolls and amiable conversations. In stark contrast, Chamé's wife had quarrelled with him and left for her parental home. Even after all this time since their wedding, he had yet to hear a kind word from her.

Adding to his woes, his sole buffalo had grown unapproachable following his wife's departure, leaving him without even the buffalo's companionship. The buffalo's antics had even led to Chamé receiving a slap from Kokalé. If not for the landlord's fear, he would have gladly pushed the stubborn creature over a cliff. Neglecting his chores was not an option, as it would result in hunger.

He pondered that it might have been better to cover himself in ashes and adopt the life of a *jogi*[4] rather than endure such a damned existence. However, becoming a *jogi* posed its own challenges, as he would have to wander from house to house, disturbing the dogs, or else go hungry. Moreover, in modern times, people would likely mock a plump, well-fed *jogi*, accusing him of choosing this path to evade the labour of tilling fields. Embracing the life of a *jogi* would likely mean residing in makeshift shelters along the waysides. In the event of falling ill, there might be no one to offer even a single drop of water. Regardless of whether people sought blessings or not, the *jogi* would instinctively step forward and intone 'Namo Narayaña, my child,' before continuing his journey, carrying a large alms bag and constantly anointing himself with ashes. Only from a distant vantage point did the *jogi's* existence seem soothing—particuarly to a man who felt the searing heat of worldly troubles.

---

[4] A male member of a religious order that originally relied solely on alms.

V

During the first week after his wife's departure, Chamé found himself irked even by the mere mention of her name. However, as time passed, an emptiness began to seep into his life. He ruminated, "She could be a bit cheeky, sure, but she had quite a lively spirit. When she set her mind to it, she'd gather enough fodder to fill the buffalo to the brim. Morning and evening, she would cook meals for me, but since she's gone, I've barely cooked anything myself—just getting by on roasted corn. When she was around, the buffalo gave plenty of milk because she took care of the milking herself. Now, it's become jumpy and uneasy. Even Juthe's wife and everyone else keeps telling me to bring her back. Whether she's willing or not, I guess I should at least try to bring her home."

The following day, after his morning repast, Chamé prepared to visit his in-laws' home. He carefully chose his finest attire, a flannel *daura-suruwal*[5], and put it on. To his dismay, he noticed that Gauñthali must have carelessly placed some tobacco on his hat, leaving a stain and causing the fabric to wrinkle. Chamé's anger flared up.

"Look at that bitch!" he fumed. "If only she had decent eyes to see the worth! Had her father or grandfather ever worn a felt hat like this, she might've understood. But her father walks around in a rustic hat and a cloak made of nettle cloth—how could his daughter have any class? What's a cow supposed to do with a nutmeg!"

He rambled in frustration for a brief period, then quickly dusted off his hat and placed it on his head. With no spare waistcoat available, he wore the same old one. He draped his cloak over his back in a bundled fashion and set off, clutching a

---

[5] The traditional Nepali male outfit includes a Daura (a type of Kurta) and Suruwal (trousers).

tattered umbrella.

Stopping to rest at a *chautara*[6] near his in-laws' home, Chamé wiped the sweat from his forehead. Meanwhile, from the outskirts of the forest uphill from the village, the sound of Gauñthali's singing reached him. She had stopped there to take a break before descending with a bundle of grass. Her song floated through the air, "I yearn to fly, yet I am not a bird, I no longer wish to stay here."

Chamé clenched his teeth in frustration and muttered, "My poor buffalo's starving, its belly grumbling like a folk singer's fiddle strings! And here she is, ringing the entire forest with her songs!"

After a brief respite, Chamé ambled slowly up the hill. As he neared the needlewood tree, a sense of reluctance crept into his steps, making him wonder what his in-laws might say. Gradually, he reached the gate and saw his mother-in-law beside a pile of refuse, scrubbing a pan. His father-in-law lounged on the veranda, calmly smoking a hookah.

Chamé joined his palms together and offered a bow in greeting to his mother-in-law, who reciprocated the gesture despite her soiled hands. He then walked up to the veranda, where his father-in-law asked him to hold his pipe and leaned forward to touch his feet in a gesture of respect. Chamé tightly pressed his feet together, facilitating the act.

Before long, Gauñthali arrived, carrying a bundle of harvested grass. She was dressed in an elegant flannel blouse and a chintz skirt, gathered in folds at her waist. Bangles adorned her wrists and a coral necklace graced her neck. Her bust was ample, and a large vermilion tika gleamed on her forehead. A rhododendron flower decked her hair, and she exuded a dusky yet exquisite allure. Chamé found immense

---

[6] A rest stop along rural Nepali foot trails, built from stacked stones with banyan or peepal trees for shade.

satisfaction in her presence, feeling as though the goddess Lakshmi herself had graced the household!

As evening darkness settled in, Gauñthali showed up and reverently touched Chamé's feet in greeting. Chamé was filled with elation. He felt a strong urge to embrace her tightly and shower her with kisses, but she gently rebuffed his advances and withdrew into the house.

Following the evening meal, a quilt was laid out on the veranda for Chamé. He stretched out, but sleep eluded him entirely. He lay there, waiting in anticipation for Gauñthali's arrival. The meal concluded, and the kitchen chores were over. Eventually, someone climbed the stairs, holding a wick lamp. Suddenly, the door was closed and locked from inside, leaving Chamé gaping in disbelief.

Chamé's mind was a tumult of thoughts. He mused, "Damn! Why did I have to blow up at Gauñthali that day? Women love going to weddings, and she's still young—what's the big deal if she wanted to stay a bit longer? Who am I to punish her for having a good time? Hitting her just because dinner was late—that's just terrible. Maybe her attitude came from how I treated her. If she comes back, I swear I won't do that again. I'll treat her even better than my brother Juthé treats his wife, just wait and see." His mind was in utter turmoil, and to add to his distress, the fleas underneath were biting relentlessly!

Early the next morning, Chamé heard the creak of the door opening. He perked up his ears, wondering if Gauñthali had shown up. But soon he realised it was his elderly father-in-law, emerging to relieve himself in the open. Chamé, meanwhile, hadn't managed to get a wink of sleep all night.

VI

It was morning, the time to release the cattle. Chamé's father-in-law propped against the wall, enjoying a smoke, while his mother-in-law husked maize on the veranda. Gauñthali was busy in the kitchen. With a touch of shyness, Chamé addressed his father-in-law, "It's time to start work in the fields. Please send your daughter back home."

His father-in-law cleared his throat, resting his cheek on the hookah's stem. "So, I hear you've been calling us names, saying we're beggars," he said. "We may not be wealthy, but we've never begged for anything! We trusted you by giving our daughter to you. If you want her back, convince her yourself. No one's stopping you!"

Chamé forced a grin. In a while, Gauñthali finished her kitchen chores. As she prepared to head to the forest with her basket and tumpline, Chamé reached out and grabbed her by the arm.

"Where are you going with that basket? Come, let's go home!"

"I'd rather die than go home!"

"And where do you plan to go if not home?"

"I don't care; I'll go wherever I please. I'll become a *jogini*[7] and wander about!"

"Who'll gather fodder for the buffalo if you become a *jogini*?"

"Your buffalo, you'll do it!"

"Stop talking too much; come with me, quickly!"

"So you can make up an excuse and beat me again?"

"Swear I'm an outcast if I do that again!"

"As if I'd believe!"

---

[7] The female counterpart of a *jogi*; a recluse.

In no time, Gauñthali dressed herself, gathered her belongings, and prepared to leave. Her mother placed a small bundle and a jar of curd in front of her. Gauñthali picked up the bundle and started walking ahead. Chamé followed behind, swaying the jar in his hand. Along the way, they began to discuss.

"How much milk does the buffalo give these days?"

"Around four and a half litres a day."

Gauñthali sneered in response.

As the sun began to dip behind the hills, herdsmen led their cattle homeward, creating a dusty trail up the incline. Chamé and Gauñthali reached the spring, where they stumbled upon Juthé's wife descending the hill with a waterpot tucked in her basket. As her gaze fell upon Chamé, she playfully stuck out her tongue, then chuckled and said, "Well, well, it's as if we have a bride leading the way and the groom following behind, like a pair of shelducks!"

"Don't rejoice too soon, sister; another spat might arise someday—you never know!" Gauñthali replied with a grin.

"See, it doesn't take time to reconcile either! A tiff between husband and wife is nothing but a blaze in the straw! ◆

ENEMY

Bishweshwar Prasad Koirala

If anyone could be described as "the toast of the town," it would undoubtedly be Krishna Ray. At forty-five years old, Ray stood out as the most genteel person in the entire village. Over the past decade or so, he hadn't set foot outside the village—a testament to his complacent nature. Ray firmly believed that lending money often brought discord, so he refrained from doing so. However, in times of need, he consistently extended a helping hand to others, embodying the sentiment that a true friend is one who stands by you through thick and thin.

When Janak Kumari suffered the tragic loss of her only son, bystanders found themselves more deeply moved by the comfort offered by Krishna Ray than by Janak Kumari's own grief. In moments of dispute among the villagers, Ray consistently assumed the role of mediator, and his judgments were accepted without question. Rarely did Ray step outside his home, and whenever he did, it was often a sign of either a bereavement in the community or some neighbourhood discord. As a result, whenever people encountered him on the streets, they greeted him with the utmost respect.

Krishna Ray enjoyed every comfort in life, whether it was material wealth, recognition, or respect. Although he did not have children of his own, he found solace in adopting a boy who was distantly related to him, thus filling the void of parenthood.

One evening, after finishing his dinner, Krishna Ray retired to bed, intending to sleep. However, his mind soon became occupied with various thoughts. No one could label his life as unsuccessful; he had amassed considerable wealth. Unlike others, he hadn't troubled his contemporaries in his pursuit of wealth. He harboured no enemies, which greatly contributed to his sense of contentment. In his forty-five years of life, he had never made an enemy of anyone.

As Krishna Ray reflected on these thoughts, they seemed to prolong his peaceful slumber until suddenly, he was struck by a baton hurled in his direction. Fortunately, the brunt of the blow missed him, leaving him uncertain whether the assailant had aimed at him or the wall.

Agitated, Ray quickly rose from his bed, but by then, the assailant had fled. "Who could have attacked me?" he wondered. "I've never made an enemy my entire life and always avoided quarrels."

Initially, Krishna Ray found it difficult to believe that he had been attacked at all—it all seemed like a blur, almost dreamlike in his sleepy haze. However, the broken shard of the baton that had struck the wall was undeniably real. Leaning over from his bed, he picked up the fragment and examined it closely, wondering, "Who could possibly be my enemy?"

After much contemplation, Krishna Ray felt he had pieced together a clue to the puzzle. Earlier that morning, he had chastised one of his servants, Ramé, for a minor mistake. Considering Rame's brazen nature, Ray wondered if his temper might have flared, leading him to attack his master. During the reprimand, Ray had noticed Ramé's face turning red, though he wasn't sure if it was from anger. However, Ramé's anger hadn't seemed particularly intense, making it odd for such an old servant to resort to violence over a minor scolding. Ramé had endured harsher criticisms in the past without incident, so why react so strongly this time? Yet, as Ray mused, human behaviour is unpredictable. Who else could be his enemy if not Ramé?

Truth be told, Krishna Ray suspected that it must have been Balbhadra's doing, not Ramé's. Recently, Krishna had caught Balbhadra red-handed attempting to manipulate accounts to deceive his boss. In response, Krishna had humiliated him publicly. Balbhadra held high esteem in society, and the villagers respected him greatly. It seemed likely that he couldn't bear the disgrace Krishna Ray had inflicted upon him and had plotted his revenge that night.

As Krishna Ray pondered, a memory surfaced of a man who had come seeking employment just two days earlier. The man was in dire straits and had approached Ray for help. Instead of offering him a job, Ray had given him a piece of advice. During their conversation, Krishna had also used some harsh language, which the young man clearly didn't appreciate. It was evident that the youth had a strong sense of dignity and might have been deeply affected by those words, perhaps holding onto the grievance for a considerable time.

In fact, Krishna Ray had a habit that was far from commendable. Despite seeing himself as free from faults or vices, he recognised one of his greatest flaws: his tendency to offer unsolicited commands and advice to others. However, rather than acknowledging it as a fault, he clung to this habit, mistakenly perceiving it as one of his greatest strengths.

Krishna Ray had taken on the role of a mediator in numerous conflicts, a responsibility he took great pride in. The villagers trusted him implicitly and often sought his intervention whenever disputes arose. This significantly contributed to the respect he garnered within the community. However, it's plausible that this role also earned him adversaries, particularly among those who were affected by his rulings.

As an example, one particular incident from the past resurfaced in his mind. A longstanding land dispute between Govinda Pundit and Goré Jamadar, which had been simmering for some time, escalated into a physical altercation that fateful day. As usual, Krishna Ray stepped forward to mediate, expressing his habitual concern over the dire consequences of their ongoing conflict.

"Listen to me, Govinda Pundit! Listen, Goré Jamadar! What good does this quarrelling bring? Make peace among yourselves. Eat, drink, and pray in the name of God," Krishna Ray urged.

If mere advice could have resolved their quarrel, they likely wouldn't have been at odds in the first place. However, despite Krishna Ray's counsel, they remained unwilling to make peace. Consequently, as the mediator bound by his obligations, Ray had to make a ruling, ultimately siding with Goré Jamadar. In doing so, he may have inadvertently made an enemy out of Govinda Pundit.

Another instance involved a conflict between a schoolteacher and a businessman. Krishna Ray, acting as mediator, ruled in favour of the businessman. In response, the schoolteacher expressed his disappointment, "Look, Krishna Ray! I respect your decision wholeheartedly. But remember, a businessman remains a businessman. He may not be of much help later."

In any conflict, the role of a mediator is undoubtedly one of the most impartial. However, it's an inevitable truth that no mediator can fully support both parties involved. Ultimately, they must choose a side, risking the enmity of the other. Krishna Ray learned this lesson as a sudden awakening.

As his thoughts continued to race, Krishna Ray recalled a quarrel that had erupted inside a railway compartment and another incident where he accidentally collided with someone in the market, causing them to stumble and fall. He remembered occasions when he had to dismiss servants and also reflected on his impoverished yet envious brothers who resented his success. These memories stirred a sense of mistrust within him, not only towards strangers but also towards his adopted son. He couldn't shake off the fear that his son might be in a hurry to seize his property, given that even biological sons could resort to such acts.

Krishna Ray threw himself onto the bed, hoping to find some respite in sleep and forget the unsettling incident. He pondered the far-reaching implications of enmity, realising that on Earth, no one is truly a friend; everyone is a potential adversary. He contemplated how conflicts often arise from seemingly insignificant reasons. Despite not cultivating many friendships, Krishna Ray acknowledged that even with the few he had befriended, he had unwittingly given reasons for resentment. He marvelled at how enmity, like a venomous snake, could lurk within seemingly harmless things.

When the case was investigated the next day, the police inspector asked, "Do you have any suspects?"

In a grave tone, Krishna Ray replied, "Ramé, Kedar, Govinda Pundit, Kanhaiya Sir, Budhé, Leela, Pushpa Raj, Ramchandra Parajuli..." ◆

THE SWEATER

Poshan Pandey

With a playful hop and skip, Sabita approached Shanti and exclaimed, "Hey sister! Brother-in-law wants to know if you'd like to join us for a movie."

"Tell him I'm not coming!" Shanti's voice was hushed, yet carried a stern edge.

Sabita lingered for a moment, innocence etched on her face. She mused about how dull her older sister could be, seemingly unaffected by the joys of life. But really, how much older was she? Just five years. As Sabita walked away, her thoughts quietly ridiculed her sister's lack of interest.

She had barely taken a few steps when Shanti's voice called her back. "Is this invitation coming from you or your brother-in-law?" Shanti asked, wearing a smile that seemed a bit forced. This unexpected response left Sabita quite surprised.

Seating herself on the floor, she gently held her sister's lock of hair and spoke with a tone that mirrored her own sprightly nature, "I was out in the garden enjoying the sunlight when Brother-in-law came up to me and suggested we all go to the cinema together. I promised to check with you first and rushed back to ask."

The brightness on Shanti's face dissipated like dewdrops slipping from grass blades with a gentle gust of morning breeze. However, annoyance didn't lace her words this time. With a simple nod, she replied, "Alright, we can go."

"Wow, that's awesome, sister!" Sabita's delight bubbled over like a fizzy burst. Her face was an open window to her feelings. However, a nagging question remained within the recesses of Shanti's heart. Unresolved, it hung in the air, continually resurfacing to pester her thoughts.

***

Sabita had come to live with her sister Shanti a few months ago. They shared a close bond since childhood. Shanti cherished Sabita's childish and lively demeanour, often feeling an urge to shower her with affectionate kisses. Sabita, for her part, still revelled in games like blind man's buff and hide-and-seek, her playful spirit untouched by time. The only change was a subtle infusion of youthful charm, something she remained unaware of.

Shanti, however, no longer enjoyed such games. Although moments of nostalgia sometimes tempted her, her shyness and reluctance held her back. In this regard, she was just the opposite of her sister. Instead, Shanti found herself constantly mulling over her inability to win her husband's love.

Each time Sabita praised her husband and highlighted his virtues, an unusual pang tightened its grip on Shanti's heart. An odd, yet suppressed, form of jealousy towards her sister would surface—one she kept hidden, never allowing it to escape even in the heat of the moment. Instead, this unspoken feeling gradually took shape, like a spider weaving its intricate web in the dark corners of her heart.

One day, Shanti sat on the veranda, doing her hair. Before her lay a small mirror. As she gazed at her reflection, a sense of aging washed over her. Strands of hair fell as she combed through, while dandruff cascaded down, flake by flake, onto her face. She quickly dusted her face with powder, and in an instant, her faced turned as white as snow.

Just then, Sabita walked in. Her eyes were lined with mascara, and she wore a cotton *salwar*[1] paired with a spotted silk *ghaghar*[2]. Her body looked healthy and strong, with a soft blush glowing on her cheeks.

"Look, sister! Your hair's starting to turn grey," Sabita said, gently pulling a silver strand from Shanti's head and placing it in her hand.

Shanti carefully examined Sabita's hair, hands, feet—every detail—but found nothing to comment on. Her voice faded into silence. Twirling the grey strand between her fingers, she simply let out a soft, thoughtful "Oh."

"Look, Brother-in-law is coming this way," Sabita said excitedly. As Gopinath came closer, she turned to him and said fondly, "See, sister's hair is turning completely grey. Why don't you buy some oil to bring back its blackness?"

Shanti found her sister's sympathy quite irritating, and annoyance festered deep within her. She stole a quick glance at her husband and noticed his gaze fixed on Sabita's face, studying it intently.

He replied, "Alright, I'll pick one up at the fair tomorrow."

***

The atmosphere at the exhibition fair that day felt stifling,

---

[1] A traditional garment with loose-fitting trousers worn with a kameez.
[2] A long ornamented skirt or petticoat, tied with a drawstring and often hung with bells.

with crowds and bustling activities filling every corner, leaving no room for relief. A Ferris wheel spun leisurely nearby, its rotations drawing the crowd's attention. Intrigued by the prospect, Sabita expressed her desire to take a ride. Gopinath bought a ticket for her, while Shanti declined the offer.

Trying to persuade her sister, Sabita said, "Come on, sister! Let's take a ride. Why not give it a try just this once? You seem so disinterested in everything!"

"If you want to go, that's fine. After all, you have your brother-in-law with you. I'm feeling queasy, so I'll wait..."

"Let it be. There's no need to push if she's not feeling well," Gopinath interjected, finishing her sentence.

Unnoticed by anyone, Shanti let two teardrops fall to the ground. She discreetly wiped her eye and leaned against a bamboo pole. The Ferris wheel started its ascent, carrying Gopinath and Sabita aloft in its circular motion. The sight was too much for Shanti to bear; a feeling of dizziness indeed began to overtake her. She turned away and moved to another spot, her face tinged with remorse.

Shanti wandered into a crowded area, where the throngs of people swallowed her up, inadvertently separating her from Gopinath and Sabita, who were on the other side. Her eyes widened as she scanned her surroundings, her mouth dry and restlessness coursing through her.

Eventually, she settled onto a bench placed outside a shop, her attention now focused on the faces of the pedestrians. Time marched on relentlessly, its cruel feet trampling over her spirit. Her mind began to conjure various scenarios, fueling a mix of jealousy, envy, and a desire for retribution. The wellspring of her eyes had dried, replaced not by tears but by the searing heat of indignation.

"Look, sister is here, relaxing comfortably. And here we

are, worn out from searching for you everywhere..."

Sabita's voice pulled Shanti out of her reverie. She looked up, surprise evident on her face as she took in the rosy-cheeked, exuberant expressions of Sabita and Gopinath. Sabita reached into her bag and exclaimed, "Ta-da! Brother-in-law bought you hair oil to restore the blackness of your hair. As for me, I picked up some wool for knitting a sweater, a pouch of cream, and some powder. I'll show you everything once we're back home, alright?"

"That's fine. It's not possible to see everything here," Shanti replied, her eyes briefly darting toward Gopinath.

"Let's get moving; we've been here for quite a while," Gopinath suggested.

As they walked, Sabita displayed the skein of wool and asked, "Sister, can I knit a sweater for Brother-in-law with this yarn?"

"No need to ask me. Ask the person who will be wearing it," Shanti replied, irritation creeping into her voice.

***

Sabita became deeply engrossed in knitting the sweater, losing track of the passing days. As the sweater gradually took shape, a sense of accomplishment and contentment began to dance across her face.

She tried the sweater on, holding it against her chest. The embroidered flower pleased her. Following her usual habit, she dashed off to check its fit against her brother-in-law's size. On the staircase, she bumped into Shanti.

"Sister, look! Brother-in-law's sweater is almost ready. I'm going to check the fit one more time. I think the sides are a bit snug. What do you think? Will it fit him well? It should, right?"

Sabita's words spilled out in a rush, as if she had no time for anything else.

A smile, though forced, appeared on Shanti's lips. Clearing her throat, she replied, "The embroidered flowers don't look quite right. They make it seem more suited for a woman. How about giving it to me? I'll knit a new one for your brother-in-law."

"Oh, come on! You say that so casually? I put so much effort into knitting it for him," Sabita responded nonchalantly, her lips forming a faint smile while her eyebrows slightly furrowed.

Sabita hurried towards her brother-in-law's room, leaving Shanti standing there, staring blankly. As she watched her sister's daily dashes to her husband's room under the pretence of measuring the sweater's fit, Shanti's suspicions intensified. These growing doubts weighed heavily on her mind, leaving many of her nights sleepless.

Once again, Shanti struggled to sleep that night. She stirred awake three to four times, sipping water and looking at the time. At 2 o'clock, she woke up again. In the hushed stillness of the dark hours, Shanti rose from her bed and scooted closer to Sabita. The sound of Sabita's peaceful breaths stirred a smouldering sensation within her. Oddly convinced that Sabita was the cause of her sleeplessness, Shanti's fingers inched toward Sabita's neck. For a moment, the air grew heavy with an unsettling tension, although it didn't last long.

Shanti's gaze fell on the sweater resting beside Sabita's pillow. She gently picked it up, her eyes tracing the front and back pieces that awaited the join. Judging by the progress, she surmised that the sweater would be complete by the following evening. Sabita's deep commitment to knitting was evident— like a solemn pledge, a resolute dedication. Remarkably, this dedication didn't drain her spirit or render her weary; instead, it seemed to infuse her with vitality and vigour.

Shanti's thoughts lingered on the next evening when the sweater would drape over Gopinath, symbolising her relinquishment of any claim to her husband. The allure of the sweater, she reckoned, would ensnare him so completely that he might never want to part with it. Moreover, Shanti was convinced that as long as the sweater remained on his body, her own peace of mind would remain lost. A disconcerting sensation enveloped her, as if a curtain were being drawn on a grim game, and the ominous toll of a bell announcing its start echoed in her ears, sending tremors through her body.

In the wake of these thoughts, Shanti's desires became increasingly tangled. She held the sweater tightly. And, as the saying goes, prevention is better than cure, she thought—why not eliminate the problem at its root by burning the sweater before it reached Gopinath? Afterall, it was right within her grasp.

However, it wouldn't be accurate to say that Shanti, while entertaining these unsettling thoughts, lacked empathy for Sabita. As a result, her jealousy quickly transformed into something else, and she began unravelling the sweater. The process gained momentum rapidly, resembling the work of a high-speed machine, with strands of unwound wool piling up on one side.

In her haste, Shanti's hand accidentally brushed against Sabita's back. Sabita stirred awake; her gaze fixated vacantly on her sister's face. After a brief pause, she asked, her voice trembling with apprehension, "Sister, what's the matter? Why are you unknitting the sweater?"

Shanti abruptly halted the unravelling process. With a resolute tone, she declared, "This kind of sweater doesn't suit your brother-in-law. I'll knit him a different one."

Sabita's face flushed with astonishment. She replied instantly, "This one isn't for Brother-in-law; it's for you. I completed his sweater last night and already gave it to him. Go and see for yourself how perfectly it fits! He went to bed wearing the same sweater." ◆

THE SPLENDID BUFFALO

Ramesh Bikal

"There's a lot of activity at Lukhuré's place; his front yard is packed with people," Dwaréba muttered as he stood in his own yard, observing from the ridge that overlooked the area. Among the crowd, he noticed a coal-black object.

"What's that in Lukhuré's yard?" he asked impatiently, as if someone were always beside him, ready to answer or agree.

But as soon as he spoke, he turned around with a start and realised there was no one around; he was all by himself. Feeling a bit embarrassed, he called out to Rambiré Gharti, who was ploughing a section of his lower yard.

"Hey, Ramé!" Dwaréba yelled. "What's all the hoo-ha at Lukhuré's place? I can see a dark object over there—it looks like some kind of beast."

"Yes, Dwaréba! Lukhuré did mention the other day that he was buying a buffalo. Could it be that he brought it home today?"

Rambiré quickly climbed the steps to Dwaréba's house, bowed to touch the old man's feet, and then looked toward Lukhuré's house, shading his eyes from the sun with his hand.

"Yes, it definitely looks like a buffalo," Rambiré confirmed. "The jerk indeed brought it home."

"Oh, the lump actually brought a buffalo!" Dwaréba exclaimed in utter disbelief, as if the very idea of Lukhuré buying a buffalo was beyond his wildest imagination. The fact that Lukhuré had managed to bring one home was nothing short of astonishing—and even offensive. Dwaréba had always wanted a buffalo himself but had kept putting his plans off. Now, knowing that a wretch like Lukhuré had managed to do so felt like a blow to his pride. A sharp discomfort pierced his chest, as if his heart had been pricked by a gramophone needle.

"What sort of buffalo did he bring?" Dwaréba asked.

"No idea, Dwaréba. He mentioned he was willing to spend around four hundred rupees on one," Rambiré replied in a subdued voice, as if he were drifting into a deep slumber. His eyes remained fixed on Lukhuré's yard, unblinking, as though he were lost in a daydream, imagining a similar buffalo tethered to a pole in his own yard, with everyone marvelling at it.

Dwaréba's curiosity reached a fever pitch. "What kind of buffalo did he manage to get?" he muttered, his feet almost moving of their own toward Lukhuré's house, drawn by an irresistible force. "Come, let's go see what the wretch bought."

A crowd had gathered in Lukhuré's yard. Podé, his four-year-old son, was circling the buffalo, clapping his hands in excitement. From the moment he saw his father at Akuri Bhanjyang, leading the buffalo home, he had been walking on air. Before the buffalo even arrived, he had already spread the news to his friends and gathered them in the yard. As soon as his father reached home, Podé ran up to him, grabbed the cuff of his *daura*[1], and clung to him.

"*Ba*, is this our buffalo? Is it really ours?" Podé asked eagerly.

---

[1] A traditional Nepali male upper garment, similar to a kurta.

"Gopé, look at the buffalo my *Ba* brought home. It's ours! Later this evening, it'll give us a pail full of milk. Then we'll make butter—lots of butter! We can sell it at the market and buy ourselves a new *daura*! We're buying one, aren't we, *Ba*?"

"We are," his father replied. "Next time we go to town, we'll get you a new *daura*."

Lukhuré's lips curved into a sweet smile, and his heart swelled with joy. The weight of his son's persistent nagging no longer brought him bitterness or pain; the despair and self-deceit that once troubled him had vanished completely. Today, a splendid buffalo was tethered in his yard. This magnificent creature, like a wish-tree fulfilling his son's longstanding desires and dreams, stood proudly at his doorstep. Lukhuré gazed at the buffalo with deep affection and tenderness. The cool evening breeze felt like the gentle touch of fortune—like a mother's loving caress.

He approached the buffalo slowly—what a marvel it was! Its udder was large, like a huge bowl, and its smooth black coat was so polished that even flies might slip off. It had a pair of stout, stubby horns. A thrill of excitement ran through him as he caressed the buffalo fondly.

Lukhuré wasn't the only one feeling elated that day; his wife, Ghaiñti, equally was. She followed her husband's instructions without any hint of resentment, unlike usual. In the past, when Lukhuré asked for a glass of water, she would come up with countless excuses to argue. But today she brought it promptly, without even being asked. Before Lukhuré could say a word, she had already prepared fodder from aged corn flour and set it out for the buffalo. She even collected grass, packed it tightly into two baskets filled to the brim, and set it aside on the porch for the night.

Ghaiñti bustled around the house with renewed energy.

Lukhuré watched her with joy—all thanks to the buffalo. Normally, his eyes ached and his ears longed for just a smile or a kind word from her. On other days, she would argue at length over the smallest matters, mistaking kindness for hostility. The Ghaiñti of the past, known for her quarrelsome and harsh nature, was a stark contrast to the caring, generous Ghaiñti of today.

Lukhuré, pleased with his wife's transformation, wore a gentle smile. As he looked around, it felt as though nature itself was sharing in their happiness. The crimson glow spreading across the western hills, the forests, the cliffs, the hillocks, and the flora surrounding his house all seemed to reflect the joy of his family.

He had completely forgotten the fatigue from his long walk of about twenty miles, up and down. Energised like a young man, he tended to the buffalo himself. He warmed the fodder and set it aside for the buffalo, cleaned the dried dung from its flanks, and even massaged the animal with oil. After finishing these tasks, he lovingly stroked the buffalo's back, lost in his affection as if he wished to merge with it.

Meanwhile, Dwaréba entered the yard with Rambiré, joining Ghamané and Khulal, who had arrived earlier. Dwaréba examined the splendid buffalo with a sharp, predatory gaze, as if he were a vulture eyeing its prey. The others followed suit, each scrutinising the buffalo with their own critical eyes.

"Lukhuré, how much did you pay for it?"

Startled by Dwaréba's sudden question, Lukhuré, who had been absorbed in stroking the buffalo with all his heart, looked up in surprise.

"I'm sorry, Dwaréba," he said, noticing the old man standing in his yard. Quickly, he stood up, approached Dwaréba, touched his feet, and then, with a drawn-out tone, added, "Well, I paid about seventeen scores for it. Was that too much?" His eyes widened with curiosity as he awaited Dwaréba's response.

The music of unprecedented satisfaction in Lukhuré's voice and the golden dreams shimmering in his eyes did not sit well with Dwaréba. A sharp pang of discomfort hit him, leaving a bitter taste in his mouth. His face briefly contorted with displeasure, and his eyes seemed to burn with a hidden envy. However, he quickly masked these sour emotions with a veneer of polite deference.

"We can't really say whether you made the right purchase," Dwaréba said, stepping closer to the buffalo. He carefully scrutinised the animal, bending down to examine its udder and nipples, and inspecting its entire body and form. He checked its eyes and horns, noting its wide, elegant hips, the udder as large as a bowl, the thick, well-formed nipples, the smooth black coat from which even flies might slip off, and the pair of blue, innocent eyes. The stubby little horns added to its impressive, splendid appearance. As Dwaréba took in the sight, his mind seemed to cloud over, like a garment turning grey in smoke.

"I think you paid a bit too much for it," Dwaréba said. "How much milk do you expect it to produce? A large udder alone isn't enough. Its fat is useless if you can't eat its meat," he added, his eyes and nose scrunched up in doubt.

Hearing this, Lukhuré was scared out of his skin. "Why do you say that, Dwaréba?" he asked, his eyes filled with doubt and fear. He tried to read Dwaréba's face but found no trace of ill will there. The indifference in Dwaréba's demeanour seemed to linger on his lips, hidden beneath his curling moustache and flickering in his words. Dwaréba cast a penetrating gaze at Lukhuré's worried eyes and then resumed his careful examination of the buffalo.

For the second time, Dwaréba walked around the buffalo. With as much sympathy as he could muster, he said, "This buffalo seems to be short-winded. Rambiré, have a look and see if I'm wrong."

Rambiré glanced briefly at Dwaréba and then circled the buffalo, inspecting its various parts. Khulal and Ghamané followed, scrutinising the animal closely. After their inspection, Rambiré spoke with a tone of resignation, "Dwaréba's eyes are rarely mistaken. He's seen many buffaloes like this one. Don't you think so, Ghamané? This buffalo does seem to be short of breath."

"Hmm..." Ghamané and Khulal both muttered in unison. It was unclear whether their response was in agreement or opposition to Dwaréba, but Dwaréba took it as validation of his claim.

He continued, "There's no chance my eyes are deceived. I've dealt with many buffaloes, and if my eyes weren't as sharp, I'd have already been done for."

Lukhuré was plunged into despair. It felt as though the planet Rahu's boundless darkness was swallowing the moon of his long-held dreams, dragging him deeper into a murky pit with nothing to hold onto. "O God!" he thought, overwhelmed and helpless.

"But Dwaréba, Jyamdi's Dhakal has promised that if there's any issue with the buffalo, he won't charge a penny for it," Lukhuré said, still trying to figure a way out.

Dwaréba's brows furrowed. "Who's that? The same scoundrel Dhakal? If you believe his words, you'll soon find yourself in trouble. He's tricked many people. Isn't that right, Rambiré? Am I exaggerating?"

"Not at all!" Rambiré Gharti replied confidently. "If this

buffalo isn't winded, you can pour ale down our gullets." He looked into Dwaréba's eyes, seeking confirmation for his strong assertions.

Lukhuré sank to the ground, cradling his head in his hands. His once-vibrant mind, like a lush garden, had been decimated by a sudden frost. The joy that had enveloped him moments ago was now replaced by a heavy cloud of distress. His eyes grew dim, and the once-cheerful sky, singing birds, and swaying vines before him now seemed to embody melancholy. Sweat clung to him, forming a sticky residue on his skin. Was it true that an earthquake had shattered the world he had carefully nurtured? Had the treasure he had valued as gold, spending money on it freely, turned out to be mere brass? Was his fate playing such a cruel trick on him? As he looked around, his house, the buffalo, and his little son Podé appeared veiled in a thick fog of despair. "Oh God," he murmured, a deep sigh escaping his lips and merging with the surrounding air.

"Damn that fraud Brahmin!" Lukhuré muttered, his voice heavy with anger and distress. "I'll haul the beast back and dump it on his doorstep tomorrow."

His son, who had been prancing around like a boss just moments before, now looked at his father with fear and confusion, unsettled by the sudden shift in mood. Ghaiñti, once full of smiles and cheer, now appeared deflated and despondent, like a waterlogged dung cake. She clung to one of the door frames, and Lukhuré could see that frustration and dismay were etched on everyone's faces.

Concealing a subtle smirk beneath his curled moustache, Dwaréba left for home, followed by Ghamané and Khulal. Rambiré placed a reassuring hand on Lukhuré's shoulder and said, "There's no use lamenting now. What's done is done. Seek advice from a few others." With that, he too departed.

Left behind were the disheartened house and its small family, steeped in frustration.

That evening, the buffalo produced very little milk, which was hardly surprising given its long, exhausting journey of ten miles. Yet, this minor setback only intensified Lukhuré's doubts. If the buffalo weren't flawed, why was the milk so scant? The incident seemed to reinforce his suspicions.

Lukhuré tossed and turned in bed all night, every part of his body aching as though stung by a thousand hornets. His little son's dreams, carefully nurtured day and night, had crumbled. On top of that, a significant amount of money had been squandered. If the money had been his savings, it might have been different. He knew money was like dirt—earned by one and spent by another tomorrow. But how many lifetimes would it take to repay the debt he owed to Nepal Bahun?

Lukhuré spent the night in torment, tossing restlessly. In the darkness, the sum of two hundred and forty rupees seemed to morph into Nepal Bahun, dancing mockingly before him. This figure, black as iron with long claws extending from his fingers, slowly reached out toward him.

A shrill cry, mingled with a strange, anguished sigh, escaped Lukhuré's throat. Instead of evoking sympathy from Ghaiñti, his cries only fueled her anger. "Serves you right, you dumb fool!" she shouted. "What would it have cost to consult a few knowledgeable people? You wasted all that money, didn't you? What a muddlehead you are!"

Ghaiñti, who had been like a goddess of love and compassion until dusk, now embodied a fierce figure of fury. She had been so thrilled about having their own buffalo that she had given away her ear and nose rings. Now, faced with such a massive debt, her anger was palpable:

"You've handed our home over to the moneylenders," she

fumed. "And on top of that, you made me part with my rings! And what did you bring home? A piece of junk! Return this carcass to its owner; fling it back at his doorstep first thing tomorrow. You blind fool!"

Staggering, Lukhuré rushed into the shed, placing the oil lamp in a wall alcove as he looked over the buffalo. It was still there, tethered to the pole, looking as black and smooth as ever. Its udder remained large and round, like a huge bowl, and its coat was so smooth that flies could slip off. The stout, stubby horns and the blue, innocent eyes were unchanged. A deep, but cold sigh of relief slipped from his lips.

Yet, Dwaréba's words echoed in his mind: "This buffalo seems to be short-winded... there's no chance my eyes are deceived... I've dealt with many buffaloes..." The idea of Dwaréba being wrong seemed implausible. Lukhuré remained deeply troubled, with uncertainty gnawing at him.

He returned to his bed, but restlessness was his only companion. The night was filled with a deep unease, exacerbated by Ghaiñti's harsh words that seemed to tear his heart apart.

"You fool! What will you do if the buffalo dies? You wasted a huge sum on a sick animal," she said, her voice dripping with scorn. Lukhuré's mind was plagued by doubt. The whispers of the wheezy buffalo haunted him, and he feared that it might collapse and die while still tethered in his yard.

In his restless state, Lukhuré would often rise and head to the shed. There, he would carefully inspect the buffalo, running his hands over its dark, smooth body, its udder as large as a huge bowl, its stout, stubby horns, and its wide, elegant hips. He would gaze into its innocent blue eyes, seeking solace in its presence. Then he would return to his bed, only to be met with Ghaiñti's harsh words, which sliced through his anxiety like a blade. In the darkness, he would turn toward his wife, his eyes filled with remorse and silent apology.

Ghaiñti's relentless torment was pushing Lukhuré to his breaking point. He had not invested all that money expecting a loss. It seemed as though fate was playing a cruel joke on them, with the deceitful Dhakal having led him astray. Why couldn't Ghaiñti see the reality of their situation?

In his desperation, he implored, "Oh God! May that imposter be reduced to ashes. He has brought nothing but tears to a poor man. A poor man's money never finds peace. Oh, Mother Goddess!"

"People in glass houses shouldn't throw stones! Do you really think you can sell this carcass and make him pay for all that happened? You fool!" Her voice, heavy with sickness and anguish, left him feeling desolate.

Lukhuré felt trapped. Returning the buffalo was a daunting task—ten miles to cover, with the risk of being turned away by its owner. Moreover, the cash he had paid was already in his grasp. If he were truly kind-hearted, he wouldn't have deceived in the first place."

Suppressing his sorrow, Lukhuré lay in bed, feeling as though he were already a dead man.

***

The following morning, the senior men of the village gathered at Dwaréba's veranda, a common practice where villagers assembled at the homes of the affluent to smoke, converse, and share their joys and sorrows. As they discussed the latest events, Lukhuré arrived with a crestfallen expression. With a heavy heart and visible apprehension, he bowed at Dwaréba's feet and settled in a corner, overcome by fear.

"What's wrong? What news have you brought, Lukhuré?" Dwaréba's sharp voice sliced through the air. "Did the buffalo give milk as usual last evening?"

"No, it didn't, Dwaréba! How could it?" Lukhuré responded, his voice steeped in defeat. He had reached the depths of his frustration.

"Didn't we warn you?" Dwaréba retorted, then addressed the gathering. "Lukhuré here is naive! That scoundrel who came here after finishing all of Madhesh is nothing but a swindler; he deceived this fool. And this fool, for his part, was too careless to investigate properly before spending such a large sum of money. We were right here in the village, after all."

Having said this, Dwaréba took a long drag from the pipe Kanchhi Ghartini had just handed him, sending clouds of ash into the air.

"You're right," Budhathoki chimed in, glancing at Lukhuré's dejected face. "This is a classic case of how good sense can go astray in tough times. Who in their right mind would spend money on a sick beast?"

"Exactly," Dwaréba agreed, turning away from Lukhuré with a gesture of contempt. "Show me a bigger fool than someone who pours all his money into such a hopeless case."

"Perhaps you took out a loan," Ghamané remarked.

Sitaram Pundit, Dwaréba's family priest, wiped his palm across the tip of his nose and declared in a stretched tone, "If his buffalo isn't sick, you can feed us filth." He then looked at Dwaréba for approval. Despite never having seen Lukhuré's buffalo, he eagerly joined in the chorus of criticism. In his zeal to please Dwaréba, he would criticise even the newest Rolls-Royce bought by Tilakram Marwari from Bombay, let alone a village buffalo.

These relentless attacks, both grounded in truth and

exaggeration, extinguished any remaining hope in Lukhuré's heart. Overwhelmed by despair, he cried out, "Dwaréba, I'm drowning in misery. That scoundrel has ruined me. I'd be better off becoming a *jogi* and leaving home forever, Dwaréba!"

"There's no point in lamenting now. Your own decisions led you to this misery. We have no part in it. Why come to us now?" Dwaréba's words were cold and unforgiving.

Overcome by deep emotion, Lukhuré fell to his knees and cried out, "Dwaréba, I've dug my own grave. What should I do now? I can accept the loss of my wife's rings as my own bad fortune. But what about the two hundred and forty rupees I borrowed from Nepal Bahun? Oh God, what am I to do?" His voice trembled, reflecting the depth of his anguish. "Oh God, what shall I do?" he repeated.

Rambiré, who had been quietly standing in a corner of the veranda, finally spoke up, "There's no other way out. You should take the carcass back to its owner."

Dwaréba roared in response, his voice cutting through the air, "Rambiré! You fool. You talk nonsense, like water slipping off arum leaves." He dismissed the suggestion with a wave, and continued, "You don't know how wicked that parasite is. Once you're in his clutches, why would he easily give your money back? He'll have you spinning in circles."

Lukhuré, his voice full of despair, cried out, "Dwaréba, I am finished. What should I do now? I've fallen into a dark pit," he lamented, writhing like a fish stranded on the riverbank.

Rambiré, pretending to be Lukhuré's closest ally, said with an air of concern, "Yes, you're in trouble. But what will you do now?" His voice was laced with feigned sympathy as he added, "Dwaréba, we should forget all other options. This poor Lukhuré is one of our own folks, after all. He's in a dire situation. If you don't help him, who will?"

Dwaréba, however, was unmoved. "What are you saying, Rambiré? Should I throw myself into the pit to save him?" His voice carried the weight of indifference.

"That's not what I mean, Dwaréba!" Rambiré quickly clarified. "Fifty or a hundred rupees might not mean much to you, but for a poor man like Lukhuré, it's enough to ruin him."

Budhathoki, eager to support Rambiré's suggestion, chimed in, "Indeed! You should help him out of this mess. He's a poor orphan who even licks your feet."

Dwaréba pondered for a long moment, his face grave, as though the weight of the world rested on his shoulders. When he finally spoke, it was with an air of solemnity, as if he were about to bestow upon Lukhuré a favour so grand that it would take lifetimes to repay.

"Do you all suggest the same thing?" he asked, glancing at the men around him. "If that's the case, I have no objections. I can do it as an act of charity. However," he paused, letting the word hang heavy in the air, "there's one condition: Lukhuré must bring the price down by fifty or a hundred rupees. Only then can I consider buying his buffalo. Otherwise, I risk financial ruin. If this act of mercy can ease a poor man's suffering, I'm prepared to do it. What do you say, Lukhuré?"

"Dwaréba has spoken wisely. Spending money on such a buffalo is like throwing it away on a carcass. Lukhuré would do well to write off this much money." This extended comment came from Pundit Sitaram. As the village's religious intermediary, his words carried the weight of scriptural authority. It was as if he were the chairperson of the meeting, and his words were final.

"See, even our respected Punditji shares the same view. What do you have to say now?" Rambiré asked, turning toward Lukhuré.

"Speak your mind, Lukhuré," Dwaréba urged, his gaze sharp and intense.

What could poor Lukhuré say in such a situation? His words had dried up, leaving him with nothing but a vacant stare as he glanced at the faces around him. The silence in the air was palpable, with everyone, except for Dwaréba, Budhathoki, Rambiré, and the Pundit, remaining silent. Their heads hung low, weighed down by the helplessness they felt, unable to bear the anguish reflected in Lukhuré's eyes.

By evening, Dwaréba's front yard was bustling with activity. The splendid buffalo, with its smooth black coat and an udder as large as a bowl, stood tethered to a pole on one side. Half a dozen of Dwaréba's children eagerly gathered around it. Dwaréba himself attended to the buffalo with the enthusiasm of a young man in his twenties.

As Dwaréba fed rice husks to the buffalo, he lifted his head and looked toward Lukhuré's yard. It was devoid of any activity. Lukhuré and his son stood quietly in one corner of the yard.

At that moment, Rambiré arrived and bowed at Dwaréba's feet. "Isn't the buffalo a gem? What do you think, Rambiré?" he asked with an air of satisfaction.

"It is, Dwaréba. It truly is one in a million," Rambiré replied. Both men then turned their gaze toward Lukhuré's yard.

Lukhuré and his son, their silhouettes gradually engulfed by the encroaching darkness from the hill, once again stared at the splendid buffalo. ◆

NO ROSE WITHERS HERE

Parijat

For the first time, I call her "Ikebana," and she enters my room with a smile. I point to the flower she arranged in the porcelain vase two days ago and explain, "Ikebana represents the art of flower arrangement, deeply rooted in Japanese philosophy. One can even pursue a doctorate in this art. In Japan, life is viewed as transient, existing only in the present and disappearing the next. They accept destiny as inevitable, rejecting the concept of sudden death. It's intriguing how geography plays such a crucial role in shaping this perspective."

She listens intently, her focus unwavering as I continue, "In a country constantly rattled by earthquakes, people don't even notice the tremors as they come and go. Many lose their lives to these recurring disasters, and it's nearly impossible for them to mourn every time over such common tragedies. This outlook on the fleeting nature of life has given rise to the art of Ikebana. Interestingly, the Japanese, in a way, prefer to choose death by *hara-kiri* over falling into the hands of their enemies in war. Since you've only recently started your journey with Ikebana, you might not yet grasp all its nuances. Honestly, I don't know much either, but today I've tried to interpret this flower arrangement in my own way. Perhaps it carries a different meaning than what Ikebana traditionally conveys."

Once again, her attention is drawn to the vase. I elaborate, "The needle-shaped leaves of the snowdrops in the background symbolise the enduring aspect of life, their evergreen nature. The pair of half-blooming roses represents a romantic couple; as they wither, they remind us that no rose stays fresh forever—signifying life's transient beauty. The solitary snowdrop on the right, pure as snow, stands for reverence and trust in love. And at the base, the slender green leaves of the Easter lily vine weave through the arrangement, representing the subtle, unseen joys of youth—much like the fragrance of the flower, these joys too fade with time."

Surprisingly, she looks at me and remarks, "You've interpreted it so beautifully. Honestly, I hadn't thought of it that way while arranging; it just looked lovely, so I kept it, that's all!"

Staring at the thoughtfully interpreted flowers for a while, she picks up the wilted rose and continues, "Yes, I may not know much about life, but I can feel that youth is fleeting. Still, I'm not inclined to accept life solely as destiny."

She giggles and adds, "It's quite ironic, isn't it? I'm drawn to Ikebana, yet today the doctor advised me to stay away from flower brambles because they could trigger allergies and worsen my itching."

"That's unfortunate. What's your plan now?" I ask.

"I don't mind," she declares, grabbing a small pair of scissors and heading outside. Moments later, she returns with an armful of weeds, leaves, twigs, thorns, and flowers.

While she's busy, I find myself drawn to a green creeper with tiny leaves entwining a withered twig, displayed in another vase. The green creeper seems to symbolise hope—no matter how harsh or worn life becomes, hope endures. This interpretation, however, may not be present in Ikebana.

Suddenly, she lets out a scream and jumps up, scattering the weeds and foliage all over the floor. I ask, "What happened?"

She points to a fully bloomed white rose and exclaims, "There, a caterpillar...." as she shakes her fingers vigorously, trying to remove it.

I notice a black caterpillar firmly attached to the rose, seemingly unwilling to come off. "Look, it's already making me itch," she says, scatching her hands and feet.

After a while, as she settles back down, I ask, "What do these white roses mean to you?"

"I suppose white roses are universally seen as a symbol of purity, right? But I don't really know much about it." She hesitates to remove the caterpillar, and the insect clings stubbornly to the rose.

I continue, "Whether you agree or not, I've interpreted it differently. That white rose represents the body of a virtuous being—and by virtue, I mean a hardworking individual. So, the rose symbolises toil, while the black caterpillar represents a force that drains the life and labour from them. A mere disturbance won't dislodge the insect. It takes real courage to remove it from the rose. Just like you are hesitating now... yet your courage alone may not be enough."

She laughs and remarks, "Oh God! Do you interpret everything in life this way? Is there nothing beyond the exploitation of labour? Is life really that dull?"

I join in her laughter and respond, "Life isn't dull; it's a feast for the caterpillars. There are many faceets to life, no doubt, but at its core, labour and exploitation play a significant role."

After a brief silence, she suddenly speaks up, "I plucked the other rose in vain; it has also been eaten away from the middle by the caterpillar. I didn't inspect it carefully."

A moment later, she screams and jumps again. I watch in surprise as it turns out that a leech has attached itself to her foot and is feeding on her blood. In a panic, she removes the leech with a pair of scissors.

Once the second wave of fear subsides, I summarise the entire experience, "Ikebana isn't as easy as it seems; I find the process challenging. It's not just about arranging flowers as it's often portrayed. They say that the philosophy of Japanese lifestyle is embedded in Ikebana. I'm beginning to feel that our lives are also trying to adapt to a similar philosophy. However, geographically, we don't belong to the race of people living over active volcanoes."

She gazes at me in astonishment and says, "Your words are not quite clear to me."

"It's quite simple," I become emotional and continue ranting, "Even the lives of our own people are fleeting; they are here today and gone tomorrow. Sons who venture to foreign lands with promises of returning home after earning money never make it back. Our brave youths, sold for dollars, pounds and rupees, are stationed at the borders and perilous regions of other countries, ready to either kill or be killed. Their lives, too, seem to exist today—can't say about tomorrow! Even without experiencing the tremors of earthquakes, our lives are so unpredictable. Nowadays, Nepali girls vanish from the fields and wilderness, never to return. They seem to be here today and gone tomorrow—so uncertain! See how Ikebana, a symbol of transient life, mirrors the philosophy of our existence?"

She leans down, trying to remove the caterpillar with the scissors. The caterpillar falls from the flower, but what about from life? A formidable question looms before me. I see the flower girl as a living question mark.

I call her over and direct her attention to the view through the window. "I don't think you can see clearly from here. Look at those hills. Do you see that raw-bricked house among them? It looks like a mole on a beautiful face, doesn't it? That house was destroyed by yesterday's rains. An old woman used to live there, whose son was killed years ago in the war."

In a flabbergasted manner, she asks, "What happened to the old woman?"

"Nothing much. A rafter happened to prop up diagonally above her, and fortunately, she survived," I continue, "She came here crying this morning. She said the house wasn't hers, and it would have been better if she had been crushed under the roof. At least she would have met her son sooner, rather than being alive to face more troubles... and so on. How uncertain her son's life was, and so is hers! Life exists one moment and extinguishes the next. Yet, we aren't like those who, having experienced the tremors of earthquakes, have internalised the natural terrors."

She focuses on the scattered flowers and leaves, appearing sombre. There are still things to be said, so I continue, "Do you know about the mother whose soldier son was killed in Nagaland a few years ago? She still has one son in Hong Kong. But she lives with her widowed daughter-in-law. Nowadays, she carries one grandson on her back and the other against her chest, spending her days crying and preparing meals for them. Her daughter-in-law goes out to earn a living—how uncertain the life and how uncertain the future!"

We both fall silent for a moment. In a subdued and disheartened tone, she says, "Time may heal the deepest wounds of the heart, but we haven't created a conducive environment for those solitary lives."

Somewhere deep within, my heart tightens, and I suddenly exclaim, "Ikebana, no rose blooming on this earth is spared—not one. All are devoured by caterpillars. Here, no rose withers on its own; instead, tears of insecurity and uncertainty glisten in everyone's eyes. The youths, sold for dollars and pounds, are not merely helpless—they are losing their potency. We, confined to our houses, are not helpless either; we are becoming cowards. We are the sinners, Ikebana—sinners! There is no doubt that these unchecked tears will drown us one day. When have we truly felt the tremor of an earthquake? Why is this uncertainty growing? The fleeting nature of things can't define our lives. What is happening to us?"

We both gaze at each other. Perhaps, we see a vacant question mark in each other's eyes. ◆

ANNAPURNA'S FEAST

Manu Brajaki

He arrived with two kilos of fish. By the time he reached home, it seemed as if he had rushed the entire way. After all, how often can you pass off buffalo meat as goat meat? So, today he bought fish at 60 rupees per kilo—since fish is considered auspicious on special occasions.

"Annapurna, Annapurna! Look what I've brought today."

Annapurna showed up—looking like the grand ruins of an edifice. There might have been beauty once, but now it's just a memory. Yet, whatever remains is still appealing, as her youth hasn't entirely faded. Like a flash of lightning briefly illuminating a chamber of the ruin, she flashed a quick smile to welcome her husband. Her round, sallow face lit up, though her husband didn't notice.

But she did notice—the four black fish in the plastic bag in his right hand. Who knows what's in the bag he held in his other hand?

"Why did you bring so much fish?" she asked, fluttering her eyes.

"We're having a feast today," he replied, handing her the

bag of fish. "We'll also be doing *Deepawali*[1] in the evening," he added, retrieving a bundle of candles from another bag and placing them on the table. From the same bag, he also took out two bottles of homemade liquor, put them in the cupboard, and remarked, "Today, we're celebrating."

Turning back to his wife and noticing her fluttering eyes, he asked, "Wait, were you asleep?"

"Why would I be sleeping in the early evening? I was sewing your trousers."

"Trousers?" He suddenly recalled the events of the previous day.

Yesterday morning, while buying vegetables, the shopkeeper—a woman more attractive than his wife—had smiled at him. He responded with an even broader smile, savouring the sweetness of her smile. When he returned home, he found Annapurna smiling too. Her smile, though without any obvious reason, startled him.

"What's going on? Why are you smiling like that?" he asked, bewildered.

Annapurna, fluttering her eyes, burst into laughter. "What kind of person are you! You should pay more attention when you dress. First, you've worn your trousers inside out. And to top it off, the seam on one of the legs has come undone from the hip to the knee, exposing your thigh."

At that moment, the shopkeeper's smile no longer felt sweet like chocolate; instead, it was as if he had bitten into a piece of chilli. He realised how ridiculous he looked, having been caught up in endless doubts and anxieties while waiting for the new constitution.

But eventually, the constitution arrived just as expected.

Back in the present, he told his wife, "Forget about it. Why

---

[1] Deepawali involves lighting candles, lamps, or lights to mark a celebration or auspicious occasion.

strain your eyes? We'll get a new pair of trousers." His gaze then shifted to her clothes. The woman who had once been full of youth and beauty now appeared like a ruin covered in cobwebs. Her face, once the most pristine chamber in these ruins, was now dusty, devoid of decoration, colour, or adornment. Even the bright, patterned curtains were gone. Everything was as barren and desolate as the Terai jungle that the Gurkhas had heroically cleared.

As these thoughts crossed his mind and he was about to speak, Annapurna interrupted, "Do trousers just appear on their own? The interim government isn't handing out trousers to everyone, is it? And how did you manage to bring all these things?"

"He-he-he, don't be upset. I borrowed a little and took some on credit. I promised my friends a feast once the new constitution arrived. You're the one who makes it all happen. That's why I call you Annapurna[2]!"

Her real name isn't Annapurna. According to her horoscope, she was named Dolkumari. Due to her round face, she was nicknamed Dalli. But because of her skill in managing the household, her husband gave her the name Annapurna. Little did he know about the glares and harsh words she endured, or the unwelcome sympathy she encountered while borrowing or negotiating loans and credits in the neighbourhood. Despite this, she didn't want to upset him today. So, with a smile and fluttering eyes, she asked, "How many people are coming?"

"Hey, you're not upset? Today is indeed a happy day! Only four people are coming. Fry one kilo of fish and make curry with the other kilo to go with rice."

"And the remaining kilo?"

[2] In Hindu culture, Annapurna is revered as the goddess of food and the kitchen, and it is believed that she ensures her devotees are never without sustenance.

"All we have is two kilos in total."

"I asked because you talked as if we had a lot more."

"Today is a feast! So I thought, why talk about the usual small amount? Besides, this feast is yours—Annapurna's feast."

Dalli, alias Dolkumari, whom her husband lovingly called Annapurna, thought to herself—"What a naive man he is! Fish isn't like other meat that's ready to cook as soon as it's brought. By the time it's prepared, two kilos will shrink to just one and a half." But she kept her thoughts to herself, not wanting to dampen his spirits.

Her husband, still cheerful, added, "And look, Annu, this rag of yours won't do for today."

Noticing her saree and blouse, which were torn and patched in places, he hesitated, his sinking heart struggling to find the right words. "Take out the saree and blouse you wore for *Teej*[3]. Go wash up and change your clothes first. It's already five o'clock; the guests will be here by six. We need to at least maintain our dignity."

Just then, their seven-year-old daughter and five-year-old son came running, excitedly shouting, "Dad brought fish! Dad brought fish!" as they began pulling the fish out of the bag.

Hearing her husband's words, Annapurna glanced at him briefly, then quickly snatched the fish from the children's hands and headed toward the kitchen.

He gleefully whistled as he began changing his clothes.

Before six o'clock, his friends arrived. The smell of fried fish wafted from inside to the outside. The kids had already lit candles and placed them on the windowsill. After all, it was their future that was going to shine brighter.

Santosh Bhattarai shook hands and remarked, "Oh man, what's that tempting smell?"

[3] Teej is a Hindu festival for Nepali women, celebrated with fasting, prayers, and dancing, often in red attire, to seek marital bliss and prosperity.

Gyanuwakar shook hands and added, "There must be another aromatic liquid to go with it!"

Bimal Nibha shook hands and said, "I'll just have the fish curry."

Kishore Nepal shook hands and joked, "In that case, let me have the biggest share of the people's movement."

All four laughed heartily. Yet, suppressing his laughter, he said in a rather sombre tone, "If only Kumud Devkota were here today; it would've been so much fun. But that guy was just as unpredictable—he left whenever he felt like it. Then again, to be fair, he didn't ask anyone before coming either."

Everyone settled down in what they called a lounge—a simple setup of a mat on the floor with a rug on top, a sheet over the rug, and a layer of cushions where they all sat.

When Annapurna realised the guests had arrived, she entered the room, smiling with fluttering eyes as she greeted everyone. They all remarked, "Oh, *bhauju*⁴, you've gained some weight." He, too, noticed that Dolkumari, a.k.a Dalli, had put on some weight. Understanding that his friends meant "you look good" by saying "you've gained weight," he also saw his wife as beautiful. Indeed, a wife appears more beautiful when seen through the eyes of friends. So, every husband should appreciate this subtle favour from his friends.

Soon, a platter of fried fish arrived, and he pulled out a bottle and glasses from the cupboard. The evening kicked off with fried fish and liquor. For a while, the conversation revolved around a debate—should they welcome the multiparty system and the constitution, brought about by the martyrs of the people's movement, with liquor? By the time the debate reached any conclusion, they had already finished two shots each, so it got resolved in a typical Nepali style.

Politics then took centre stage.

⁴ A term used to refer to a friend's wife, translated as sister-in-law.

"*Prajatantra*[5] means..."

"Wait, are we still *praja*? Better call it *Loktantra* or *Janatantra*[6]..."

"Meaning *Naya Janavad*..."

"Not *Naya Janavad*, it's *Naulo Janavad*[7]..."

"Marxism is dead..."

"Philosophy doesn't die. It's a chain of human thought..."

"Come on, even a dead elephant is worth over a lakh now..."

"Can these feudal customs be called democratic?"

"Feudalists who are also democrats..."

"Can we get some more fish, *bhauju*? It's yum..."

"Gramsci once said that..."

"Bernstein once said that..."

"Jean-François Revel's *Without Marx or Jesus*..."

"Karpatri's *Marxism and Ramrajya*..."

"Where did Euro-Communism go?"

"Pan-Islamic Organisation..."

"Ah, the fish is so delicious! Some more, *bhauju*..."

"Oh, Santosh Bhattarai is starting his drunken rant..."

"Gyanuwakar looks exactly like Johnny Walker..."

"Look who's talking!"

"Well, Bimal Nibha is already drowned in the fish curry..."

"And this mediocre journalist, Kishor..."

"Forget it... let's drop this topic..."

"The blood of the martyrs..."

"Pour more liquor, man, if there's any left..."

"*Bhauju*, some more fish, please..."

Their son and daughter stood on either side of the doorframe, peering into the room as if glimpsing the future—

---

[5] "Praja" is people and "tantra" is rule, meaning 'people's rule' or 'democracy.'

[6] *Loktantra* and *Janatantra* are modern forms of republicanism.

[7] *Naya Janavad* and *Naulo Janavad* both mean New Communism; the two friends are simply debating whether to use "Naya" or "Naulo" in their drunken stupor, both of which mean 'new.'

forgetting even to eat the fish they held. Since he had asked his wife to give them only the heads, each child had a fish head in their hands.

The political discussion continued as the third bottle arrived, courtesy of Annapurna.

"We need to run for the elections jointly..."

"But campaigning should be done in secret... just for oneself."

"Who are you voting for?" asked Gyanu.

"Who are you voting for?" asked Santosh.

"Who are you voting for?" asked Bimal.

"Who are you voting for?" asked Kishore.

"Who are you voting for?" asked He.

"Who are you voting for, *bhauju*?" asked all his friends except him.

"To whoever you suggest," replied Annapurna.

"We asked you only because we couldn't reach an agreement among ourselves. Now, this constitution grants full rights to women. Every political party must have at least five percent female members."

"I think it's time for dinner now."

Annapurna turned and headed into the kitchen. His curiosity about her response soon faded. Annapurna, who expertly managed the household, handled the situation in her usual, subtle way. It seemed all wives were like her—skilled at sidestepping direct opinions during arguments.

Lacking awareness, thought, or opinion seems almost inhuman. Is being a wife truly so dehumanising? But then, women, like men, possess a range of qualities and characteristics. Why are they relegated to the role of wives and thus deemed inhuman and heartless? Perhaps one should ask Lord Rama.

The candles had all burned out. If there had been an electric chandelier, it would have continued to provide light. Or if only they could afford a ghee lamp; if only!

The food arrived. Annapurna, with the enthusiasm of a gracious host, served everyone fish and rice with great pleasure.

While eating, Santosh suddenly shouted, "*Gurans! Gurans! Gurans!*[8]"

"What's wrong? What's wrong?" someone asked.

"Did a fishbone get stuck in your throat? It's not '*Gurans*' you need. Forget this old remedy and just swallow a plain ball of rice," came the suggestion.

After the meal, everyone began to leave, wishing for a bright and prosperous future for the country and society. Santosh Bhattarai, relieved to have safely dislodged the fishbone, shook hands. Gyanuwakar Paudel, staring at Annapurna and humming *'Khandahar naya naya'*—meaning newly renovated ruins—shook hands. Bimal Nibha, still a bit off and on, shook hands. Kishore Nepal, the so-called mediocre journalist, adjusted his tie and shook hands. Finally, everyone advised Annapurna to keep her vote secure with herself, to which she responded with a hearty laugh.

After everyone left, he poured the remaining liquor into his glass.

"Are you having more drinks?" Annapurna asked.

"Just a few. Have the kids gone to bed?"

"Yes."

"Okay, then have your meal."

Collecting the dirty dishes, Annapurna walked toward the kitchen. He began drinking, contemplating how to balance the family budget between sips. It felt like a tangled thread—pull it one way, and it knotted at the other end; shift it another way,

---

[8] In Nepali culture, saying "Gurans" (rhododendron) or eating a Gurans petal, is believed to help settle a fishbone stuck in the throat.

and a new knot formed. His thoughts became muddled with each drink, and he staggered with each step. Frustrated, he stopped trying to think. He reasoned that there was no need to strain his head while Annapurna was around. With this self-assurance, he went outside to urinate.

As he approached the bedroom, he saw that the children were fast asleep. However, when he reached the kitchen, he forgot his need to use the bathroom as soon as his eyes fell upon Annapurna.

Dalli, also known as Dolkumari but called Annapurna, was sitting on a stool among the dirty dishes, munching on a handful of rice flakes with an old lemon pickle on a saucer. She had placed a ewer of water near the saucer to rinse the sour taste of the pickle from her mouth. With her eyebrows furrowed and her focus entirely on the rice flakes, Annapurna didn't notice him.

Unable to bear the sight in the kitchen, he looked outside. The city sparkled with lights in celebration of the new constitution. Overwhelmed by his thoughts, he glanced back inside and stood there staring for a while.

When Annapurna, seeking a change of taste, licked the edge of the wok to get the last bit of fish curry, a question struck him as sharply as the fish bone: Are our wives' opinions truly secure? ◆

INJURY

Bhaupanthi

The old man Bhaskar slipped on the stairs and tumbled to the pavement, landing on both his feet and hands. For a moment, he struggled to comprehend what had just happened. His knee had struck the hard, cemented pavement, resulting in an injury, though his palms remained unscathed. He wondered how he would explain the situation to his family, as there were no visible external injuries.

Yet, Bhaskar couldn't shake the feeling that his time might be drawing near. It was as if he had been anticipating this moment, and the fall served as a foreboding sign of its impending arrival. Bhaskar always tried to maintain a clean and tidy appearance through regular showers and a strict hygiene routine, projecting an image of well-being. However, despite how neat and robust he appeared, the fall left him sprawled on the ground. His ego suffered a blow as well, as it exposed the false impression of his well-being, for ultimately, humans are mere subject to the hands of time.

Struggling, the old Bhaskar managed to rise to his feet, brushing off the dirt. Passersby strolled nearby, but those in the shops barely spared him a glance before returning to their shopping. The lack of concern from others disheartened him; an elderly man had a fall on the street, yet no one offered even the smallest gesture of sympathy or support. Doubts turned into certainties—he couldn't help but question the depth of empathy in people's hearts; it seemed to have drained away.

He found it hard to fathom the extent of people's indifference. However, he took small consolation in the fact that no one had berated him, saying, "Hey, old man! Why are you lying in the middle of the road? Move!" Although he hadn't remained sprawled on the ground for long, he did rest his face against the pavement momentarily. This act wasn't driven by an expectation of assistance in getting up; rather, he sought to gauge the extent of his injury and determine if he could stand on his own feet.

Finally, he managed to regain his footing. Curiously, no one in the vicinity showed any surprise or interest—not even a subtle acknowledgment, like the thought that even an old man can stumble like this. Among the passersby were not only youths but also fellow old people. One old man watched him with a look of helplessness from the edge of the pavement before eventually turning away and blending into the crowd.

The road was bustling with traffic, including a densely packed bus that rumbled past. While Bhaskar had no intention of boarding the bus, he couldn't help but feel that even the bus had moved past without taking notice of him. This sentiment was driven by the fact that he had taken a similar bus from his home to reach this shopping area, where the accident—so he perceived it—had occurred.

Yet, he knew he couldn't remain sprawled on the ground indefinitely. Gathering his resolve, he stood up and acted as if nothing had happened. Strangely, no one bothered to ask, "Sir, are you okay?" Despite being injured, he took a few tentative steps to assess the extent of his injuries. His knees seemed to hold up fine, and his hands appeared unharmed as well. As he did this, he unintentionally struck a dancing pose—touching his knees and hands oddly. Satisfied that everything was intact, he brushed off his clothes and checked his pocket, finding that the modest sum of money he carried remained securely in place.

Back at home, there was an underlying concern that Bhaskar, the father-in-law, might return under the influence of alcohol. However, he had no inclination to drink at the moment. He reasoned, "Why start drinking in the morning? I'd rather deliver the shopping items first and then head to the usual pub for a drink. At least that way, I can maintain my self-respect."

While his family disapproved of his drinking habits, Bhaskar believed that as long as he paid for his own booze, no one had the right to tarnish his reputation. Many had advised him against drinking in his old age, citing health concerns. Yet, he understood that the implication of "concern" was possibly an untimely demise. The inevitability of death was not a new realisation for him; it was a reality he had long accepted. However, the unexpected slip and fall earlier had now intensified his feeling that his time might be approaching.

As he stood up, dusting off his clothes, a subtle dizziness enveloped him. It wasn't a severe vertigo that could topple him again, but rather a feeling of inner turmoil, like being stirred by a churner. Almost involuntarily, he murmured, "Sooner or later, everyone must depart." Yet, what astonished him more was the nonchalant reaction of people to his fall. It seemed that they regarded such an incident as a natural occurrence for someone his age.

He positioned himself just outside the shop's vacant space, making sure not to obstruct the flow of people. He speculated that his family was likely awaiting his return at home. He could have come back empty-handed, forgoing the shopping altogether, and offered the excuse, "I wasn't feeling well, so I came back without shopping." By simply returning the shopping money, he could have avoided any potential outburst. Even his son wouldn't have to wear that displeased expression, wondering whether the old man had been drinking.

Bhaskar disliked how his son labelled him as an alcoholic. In his son's eyes, Bhaskar wasn't just a man with drinking problem; he was also seen as someone who had squandered life's opportunities. "Dad, your drunken episodes bring shame upon us. It's because of you that we find ourselves in such dire straits." His son's reproachful words echoed, but Bhaskar brushed it aside. "When have I ever indulged in behaviour that brought shame? I've provided you with an education, enabling you to secure a job. That job has sustained the family well. I've fulfilled my responsibilities." Although Bhaskar's responses held truth, his son remained unconvinced, persisting in his doubts.

In reality, the primary concern here wasn't about his son's potential reaction. What truly bothered him was the absence of even a single word of sympathy for an old man who had suffered a fall on the street. Why did people behave this way? This question gnawed at him incessantly. He recognised the need to find a remedy for this unsettling feeling and had a solution readily available. Adjacent to the grocery store he frequented was a dim, narrow alleyway leading to a pub. He decided to head that way.

Emerging from the pub later on, he found himself intoxicated. His senses were muddled, making it nearly impossible to find his way home. The thought of the shopping errand had slipped from his mind. Unburdened by fear, he stumbled around and eventually stopped in the middle of the bustling road connected to the alleyway.

Bhaskar struggled to maintain his balance, swaying unsteadily in his drunken state. Despite his condition, he tried to stand as straight as a pole in the middle of the road. This stance held a profound significance for him at that moment. Drivers in passing cars yelled at him, "Move aside, you old fool! If you're that eager to die, go drown in Vishnumati River!" It was common knowledge that the water level in the Vishnumati River was low, but who would cite verses from the Holy Gita in such an angry and chaotic situation? Motorists manoeuvred around him to continue on their way.

A short distance away, a group of young girls chuckled, hiding their laughter behind their hands, finding his behaviour utterly absurd. Bhaskar retorted, "Come here, you people! Run me over if you dare. Do you have the courage? Are you trying to oppress me? Does this road belong to your fathers?"

He continued to babble incoherently, stumbling along and occasionally placing himself in front of moving buses. The drivers, startled, slammed on the brakes as if the very road might shatter. A driver leaned out of the bus, hurling profanities at Bhaskar: "You old man! Do you want to die or something?" Although Bhaskar's question about road ownership had no real relevance, the driver misinterpreted his words and unleashed a barrage of harsh curses.

After a period of this escalating commotion, a traffic police officer arrived, punctuating the air with shrill whistle blows before grabbing Bhaskar by the shoulder. Initially resistant to the officer's attempt to guide him to the roadside, Bhaskar struggled to maintain his stance.

"I'm not arresting you! Just move to the side of the road, old man!" the officer said.

By this point, Bhaskar's intoxication had somewhat subsided. Nonetheless, he made a veiled threat to the officer, "Go ahead, take me wherever you can. All you can do is intimidate the small fish in the pond. You lack the courage to catch the big ones!"

The officer chose not to engage in a verbal exchange with Bhaskar. Instead, he simply escorted the old man to the pavement, stopped a passing bus, and made sure Bhaskar boarded it to go home. Did the traffic officer arrange a complimentary bus ride for Bhaskar just because he was intrigued by the question Bhaskar posed about sparing the larger fish? Perhaps the question would linger in Bhaskar's mind as he faced his daughter-in-law's admonishments at home.

Indeed, Bhaskar found himself contemplating—perhaps there still remains a fragment of empathy within human beings. ◆

THE PEACH TREE

Padmavati Singh

"Look, this tree will bear peaches soon," Rasmi says, pointing to the flourishing peach tree on the west side of the garden.

"Who knows when?" Muna sighs.

"The peaches on this tree will be delicious... large and quite juicy..."

"How can you say that before they've even grown?"

"You'll see!" Rasmi quickly defends, though a small part of her wonders if Muna might be right.

This is the usual exchange between the two best friends as they stroll through the garden at nightfall. Unbeknown to them, a pair of eyes watches from a window in the house across the garden.

Rasmi's grandmother suddenly pauses from prepping vegetables and examines the girls with her experienced eyes. Rasmi overhears her grandmother say to her mother, "Dear, don't you think Rasmi will start menstruating soon?"

Her mother gives her a thoughtful look, then laughs softly, as if agreeing with her mother-in-law. Rasmi feels something—

neither entirely uncomfortable nor unpleasant, but strange. This unexpected conversation tickles her from inside.

Pretending not to have overheard, she goes into the next room without any particular reason. The pleasant mood of the evening fills the space. She gazes out absentmindedly from the eastern porch, looking as far as she can see, toward the horizon. Countless tufts of clouds in various shapes drift serenely across the sky. The sunset bathes the western horizon in gold, lending an elegant, mesmerising beauty to the scene. Her eyes drink in the sight, when suddenly, they are drawn to the peach tree.

The tree is covered with buds just about to flower. She looks astonished, realising she hadn't noticed them until now.

Just then, her mother enters the room.

"Mom! The peach tree is starting to bloom," Rasmi says, brimming with joy.

"Of course! The peach tree has come of age. From now on, it will bear peaches."

"Oh, really?" Rasmi feels a thrill of excitement.

Her mother's eyes fall on the window of the house across the garden, and she frowns. "Get inside! Why are you sitting on the porch with nothing better to do than talk nonsense?"

Rasmi is surprised to see her mother's cheerful face suddenly turn sour. Trying to understand the reason, she glances quickly at the window across the garden. Even in the dim twilight, she can clearly make out a man's back framed in the window.

"He must have turned away as soon as he saw Mother," Rasmi realises, and her face flushes red as she lowers her head.

"Get inside! Bring your grandmother's prayer items upstairs," her mother says with more anger than authority.

Rasmi quietly follows her mother into the house. Her mother briefly scans her from top to bottom and adds, "I can't call you a child anymore, but you're not quite a young woman either. You don't even know how to dress properly—neither fish nor fowl!"

Rasmi feels a surge of unpleasant anger as her mother looks at her with a new outlook and a changed demeanour, nagging her without reason. Just as she picks up the prayer items and turns around in frustration, her mother, in an agitated voice, asks, "Wait a minute, have you started menstruating?" The urgency in her mother's tone stops Rasmi in her tracks.

"Let me see..." Her mother rushes toward her. "Oh... you have, after all. How could you not realise? O God!"

At this announcement, Rasmi's heart starts to pound, and she stares at her mother in shock.

"Why are you staring like a half-wit? Come here, right now!"

Her mother grabs Rasmi's hand, pulls her into another room, and locks her in. She informs Rasmi that she must not see sunlight or the face of a man for twelve days.[1] Overwhelmed by this sudden shift, Rasmi feels something inside her break, something strange happening, and is overcome with an intense desire to cry.

For a restless girl like Rasmi, who struggles to stay in one place for even an hour, spending eleven more days in the same room feels nearly impossible. The thought of it exasperates her.

As the days drag on, she sulks in the dark room, her mind racing with many thoughts.

"So, I'm a young woman now. I'm not the same as I was before. How did this change come about so quickly, and why? What will my future be like?" Her curiosity grows, stretching as

---

[1] In Nepali culture, when a girl first menstruates, she is kept in isolation for 7 to 12 days. During this time, she is often restricted from seeing sunlight and men, as it is believed that her body is undergoing a significant transition to womanhood.

wide as the sky.

"Now I must reach the sky and dive into the ocean," her inner soul seems to whisper.

As the days roll by in the dark corner of the house, her curiosity weighs on her mind, like soft cotton fluffs gently brushing against her.

"So, coincidence can be this astonishing!" she muses. "The peach tree is blooming at the same time as the flower of youth is blooming in me, in the same month of the same year..." Her sense of wonder takes root, growing steadily to great heights.

Earlier, as she gazed from the porch, drawn by the blossoming buds of the peach tree, Rasmi too had noticed the pair of beguiling eyes watching her from the house across the garden. But she had pretended not to see them. Now, with ample time to reflect, she tries to focus on those eyes and their allure. A smile plays on her lips as though she has solved a puzzle. Suddenly, she rises, as if remembering something important, spreads out various makeup items around her, and becomes engrossed in beautifying herself.

First, she braids two pigtails. Next, she carefully applies black kohl around the rim of her eyes and places a red *tika*[2] between her eyebrows. Hesitantly, she applies lipstick to her lips. She picks up a mirror and gazes at her own reflection. For a long moment, she is entranced by her own form and beauty, experiencing a sense of pride for the first time. Just then, she hears the door open and footsteps approaching. Quickly, she hides the mirror.

When Rasmi sees her mother in front of her, she stammers with the guilty look of someone caught red-handed, "None of my friends came today. Even Muna didn't show up. I felt low, so I was just putting on some makeup." She forces a smile as she

---

[2] A tika (or bindi) is a decorative mark worn on the forehead by women, especially married ones, as a fashion accessory. It comes in various colours, sizes, and designs.

explains.

But her mother's reaction isn't one of amusement. Instead, her expression gradually shifts from initial amazement to a mix of approval, joy, and envy.

"Rasmi! I really don't approve of excessive makeup," her mother says sharply.

For a moment, silence fills the room as they each get lost in their own thoughts. After a few minutes, her mother breaks the silence, asking, "Do you want some tea?"

Although Rasmi craves a cup of tea, she replies, "No."

Her mother says nothing and leaves the room. As soon as she is gone, Rasmi hurriedly gets up and locks the door. She then looks sadly at her face in the mirror and, in a fit of anger, roughly wipes off the kohl, *tika*, and lipstick. With tears streaming down her face, she thinks, "If only I could have sent my adorned self to the window next door, how enchanted he would have been."

As she thinks this, her eyes fall on her watch—it's exactly five o'clock. He is probably at the window now, scanning the porch and the garden with his gaze. Rasmi feels a pang of unhappiness. Something inside her has been stirred, as if something has spilled into her heart, and she feels a constant surge of sadness.

The sound of a bird chirping drifts into her ears from outside, likely perched on a branch of the same peach tree. Her thoughts return to the peach tree, now covered with blossoms. The image of the blooming tree, displaying its elegance and beauty from the corner west of the road, flashes before her eyes. In an instant, the tree transforms into the form of a man— broad chest, virile body, and those same enchanting eyes meeting hers. The figure smiles slowly at her.

Rasmi feels as though the figure is moving towards her

with slow, deliberate steps. She holds her breath and watches silently as those legs draw nearer. When she feels his breath gently touch her face, a wave of elation sweeps over her, as if she's been hypnotised. Overcome by shyness or some other emotion, she closes her eyes.

In an instant, he wraps her in his strong embrace, his grip tightening with every attempt she makes to escape.

"Aha! How beautiful you are. Like a flower just blooming from the bud. I've been wanting to drink my fill of you," he whispers, his mouth close to her ear.

The sound of repeated knocking on the door jolts her awake from her deep trance. She feels as if she has been abruptly thrown to the ground while climbing a mountain. Wiping the sweat from her forehead with her shawl, which has wetted her eyelashes, she opens the door.

"Were you asleep, or what? I've been knocking for a while," Muna says as she steps into the room. Rasmi doesn't respond; she just stares blankly at Muna's face.

"Why are you looking at me like that? Were you having a dream?"

"Not a dream, but something else..." Rasmi trails off, her lips continuing to move slightly.

"You are in a strange mood today!" Muna observes. At that moment, Rasmi suddenly embraces Muna and sighs deeply. After a while, she regains her composure.

"What's wrong with you? Are you unwell or what?" Muna asks suddenly.

With a faint smile on her face, Rasmi says, "Muna! The peach tree in our garden is in full bloom! Did you see it?"

"Yeah, I saw it."

"Soon it will bear fruit." Rasmi's eyes take on a dreamy look. She longs to leave this dark room and gaze at the blooming peach tree to her heart's content. She sighs, "These remaining two days feel like an eternity to me..."

The twelve days eventually pass. Rasmi now spends her evenings under the peach tree, taking a book with her and pretending to read. She starts to find divine joy in these moments. The eyes watching from the window across the garden gaze at her openly. Gradually, they begin exchanging silent smiles and gestures.

As the days go by, fruits begin to grow on the tree. With each passing day, as the fruit takes shape, Rasmi becomes increasingly impatient to taste it.

After some time, the peaches ripen, taking their final shape. The scent of ripe peaches fills the entire garden. Rasmi is constantly drawn to this scent, her desire to eat them growing stronger each day. Since the first flowers of the peach tree bloomed, her grandmother has repeatedly said, "You can't eat the first fruit from a tree in your own garden until you've offered one to the gods!" Fearful of her grandmother's admonitions, Rasmi has yet to gather the courage to pick a peach from the tree.

One day, when her mother and grandmother are out attending a devotional service, Rasmi nearly picks a peach to eat but is stopped by an inner voice that makes her withdraw her hand.

As she relaxes under the peach tree, a ripe peach falls near her feet due to the moving breeze. She picks it up and sits indecisively for a moment. Part of her urges her to give it to her grandmother for an offering to the gods, while another part tempts her to eat it in secret. Just as she is caught in this dilemma, she sees Muna approaching from a distance and quickly hides the peach in her shawl. At the same time, she notices her grandmother coming from the same direction, causing her heart to race.

Desperately, she casts a glance toward the window across the garden. As soon as her eyes meet the watchful eyes that have been following her every move, the confidence she had been losing is reignited.

She holds the peach hidden in her shawl tightly, perhaps feeling a sense of connection with it. ◆

THE ILLUSION

Ramlal Joshi

He watched as the bus sped through the pine forest. Never had he imagined that one day a bus would zoom across the crest of this hill, which overlooked the winding flow of the Seti River since time immemorial. Public transport had reached the mountains. Electricity had arrived. Mobile phones were now common in the villages. Even the most remote mountain areas had transformed.

Returning to the village after twenty-one years, he found it strangely unfamiliar. The pine forest had already become alien to him. He set the old bag from his shoulder down at the base of an old tree. The cool breeze from the rustling pines refreshed him to the core. Leaning against the tree, he felt a wave of relief. As he took the last puff of his *beedi*[1], the smoke curled around his mouth, forming clouds near his eyes before drifting up into the sky.

The desolate hills across the way, the lush green forest, and the pristine blue Seti River captivated him, making him want to keep gazing. New emotions stirred within his heart. He

---

[1] A slender tobacco-filled cigarette wrapped in a tendu leaf, originating from the Indian subcontinent.

hummed softly to himself:

"*The more it flows, the more tears fill the eyes,*
The more one cries, the more the tears arise.
The more one endures, the sorrow clings to hills,
The more it quenches, the thirst in the heart spills."

Before he could finish reading the few pages of his heart, he noticed a young woman carrying a bundle of grass on her head, her beauty rivalling that of the rhododendrons as she walked ahead. The sight of this blooming hill maiden, with her graceful stride, revived his weary body. He rubbed his eyes, and as he blinked and peered them wide, he saw—

A young woman dressed in a *gunyu* skirt, a traditional *dhaka* blouse, Chinese slippers, and a white sash around her waist. Her long braid was tied with a lace, and a rhododendron flower adorned her hair. Her clothes were slightly worn, but her large eyes, set in a somewhat sorrowful face, bore a striking resemblance to Indrā's. Before his very eyes, he saw—

Indrā, exactly as she had been when he left her twenty-one years ago. Her nose was the same, her earrings still dangling from the same two ears. The long, silky braid that had always mesmerised him was unchanged, with not a single strand fallen. He could still see her childhood habit of tying a rope around her braid and threading a ribbon through it, just as she always did. Her graceful walk was unchanged, her waist as it had been, her ample bosom the same, and her fair complexion unaltered. A new sense of vitality surged through him. Looking down with delight, he saw the Seti River flowing as it always had. And Indrā—she was just the same.

He forgot the twenty-one years of exile. Memories vividly danced before his eyes—those same days, that same life. The time he spent in Indrā's love and company after their marriage seemed to come alive again. He thought to himself:

"Even after twenty-one years, my Indrā hasn't changed a bit. Thank you, God—a thousand times over."

He felt a deep sense of contentment. He wasn't sure how many tears of joy had flowed at the base of the pine tree. As he watched, his beloved Indrā slowly faded from view. He wondered—

"Indrā looks exactly the same—could her anger be the same as well?"

He recalled that unfortunate day when, disregarding her husband's love and respect, she had said:

"Such a sinner should just leave the country."

He didn't care about society, but the sting of his wife's hatred pierced his heart deeply. That very night, he left the village.

He had no desire to light another *beedi*. As he gazed at the winding path of the Seti River, he thought—

"Seti is the same, and so is Indrā. Thank you, my God."

He found joy in gazing at the Seti and contentment in seeing Indrā. Filled with a sense of peaceful fulfilment, he arrived home. As he looked behind the house—

The pomegranate tree stood as it always had. The black plum tree remained unchanged. The branches of the peach and guava trees had begun to droop toward the ground. Hundreds of bamboo shoots had sprouted in the bamboo grove. The climbing ivy had covered the butter tree below the house. The courtyard, porch, and pavilion were all as they had been. Once again, he felt content. He thanked God—

"You've preserved my world just as it was, without destroying a single thing. My God, I bow to you a thousand times."

A gentle breeze, rustling through the tender spring leaves, seemed to coax a faint smile onto his face. In the distance, he saw a weary, frail woman carrying a load of firewood, making her slow way towards the house. He squinted and looked up from the porch, and it seemed to him that she resembled his mother.

Even back then, his mother had been like this—withered, thin, despondent, and perpetually sad. Since his father left, she had never regained any weight. She remained unchanged: her hair, rough and thin from hair loss, was tangled into small knots; her face was completely drained of its glow, painted with a bleak, sorrowful expression. Her blouse was torn in places, her saree streaked with dirt, and her slippers worn out. He looked closely—the heart-wrenching figure was indeed his mother. She looked just like his mother. His heart shattered. Yet he thought, even after her son disappeared, she hadn't lost any more flesh. She hadn't stopped carrying firewood or cutting grass. Her routine, her life, remained unchanged. He muttered—

"Thank you, God, for keeping my world unchanged."

As the frail mother-figure drew closer, he wondered, "Mother looks the same—could the fire of her anger inside still be the same?"

He recalled his mother's words from that day—

"A disgrace like you should leave the village. It's a shame to even see you alive."

He hadn't cared about the villagers' accusations, but when his own mother cursed him like that, he had left home that very night. He took a deep sigh and as his breath faded into the air, he began to reflect on the indelible scars etched in his heart—

That morning, he was on his way to meet Chandré Damai, taking the Saikharka route toward Sisnépakha. Saikharka was home to the cattle sheds of the Baidars and Talukés—the landlords. It was the season for raising buffaloes in these sheds.

From a distance, he saw a buffalo in distress—a bamboo shoot had fallen from the slope, with one end wedged on the buffalo's horn and the other still caught on the slope, forcing the animal's head and mouth to the ground. Unable to watch the creature's suffering, he rushed into the shed. Climbing onto the buffalo's back, he tried to remove the bamboo shoot from the slope. But as the buffalo shook its body, he was thrown into the dung. At that moment, Naré, who had come to milk the buffalo, saw him covered in dung. Naré, with whom he often had disputes, saw no better opportunity for revenge. Like a gust of wind, Naré raced back to the village, spreading the rumour—"He banged the buffalo..."

The Baidars and Talukés summoned the entire village for a gathering. During the assembly, he was found guilty of having intercourse with the buffalo. While he was indifferent to the villagers' accusations, the sting of his own mother's and wife's words pierced his heart. That very night, he disappeared.

For twenty-one years, he lived raising cattle for a Punjabi household in Bareilly's Parwanipur. During all that time, he never once felt the urge to return to the village. He didn't know if his mother or wife had searched for him, but he never sought them out. Detached from the world, he immersed himself in the life of cattle rearing.

Last Monday, about an hour before he awoke, he had a dream—

His mother was being swept away by the Seti River as she screamed, "Save me!" Indrā was about to leap into the water, while villagers stood by with lamps, and someone was trying to push him in as well. He woke up with a start, deeply shaken by the vivid dream. Overwhelmed by the image of his mother's face and the memories of his wife, he felt an intense urge to cry. The next morning, without a word to anyone, he packed his bag and left.

As he drowned in the bitter memories engraved deeply in his heart, the woman carrying the firewood drew closer. Setting down the heavy load, she watched him closely. His eyes drooped, weighed down by a mix of embarrassment, guilt, and shame. Yet, before the grandeur of motherhood, where would there be room for penance? Still, he tried to lift his eyes from this humbling gaze of repentance and looked at the motherly figure. The desire to see her up close as a mother filled him with immense joy.

To his dismay, the reality he had glimpsed moments ago seemed to shatter. What he had perceived as reality had been an illusion all along. God had not preserved his world; instead, transformed it into something entirely different. The woman, who had seemed like his mother, was now prostrated at his feet, crying. Through her muffled sobs, he heard her voice—

"O my lord, where have you come from? O my deity, how this life's been shattered by the schemes of enemies! Have you descended from the sky or emerged from the earth after all these years? Where did you go, leaving me to drown in tears? You didn't even come to see your mother one last time. What has brought you back today, my life?"

His sense of complete fulfilment and joy turned to ashes. The woman he had believed to be his mother was, in fact, his wife, Indrā. As he cradled Indrā's head against his chest, he gazed into the distance and saw the young woman resembling Indrā, whom he had spotted while resting under the pine tree. She was standing right at the door, fixing him with an unblinking stare.

From Indrā's face resting against his chest, he heard her say—

"Oh, my daughter Karuna, today our destiny has changed.

The broken fate has been mended. This life of mine has been renewed. Today, my God has appeared. Go, daughter, and bring the prayer plate with *tika*[2] and *akshata*[3] for the deity. We must light the lamps and perform the *arati*[4]. Hurry, my daughter Karuna, hurry."

As she spoke, tears welled up in Indrā's eyes again. Her throat tightened, and her crying grew more intense. As he lifted Indrā from his wet, tear-soaked chest, he noticed—

She was no longer the same Indrā. The serpentine braid no longer hung down her back. The pond-like eyes, the round and fair face, the beautiful lips like peepal leaves, the graceful hips, and the ample bosom—all of these features had now transferred to Karuna. Indrā had been reduced to skin and bones.

Standing at the door with all the youthful traits of Indrā from twenty-one years ago, Karuna stared at her father with unseeing eyes. After hearing her mother's lament, Karuna went inside to light the incense, but he couldn't bring himself to follow her with his gaze. In an instant, his world seemed to disappear before his eyes. ◆

---

[2] A ceremonial mark made on the forehead with coloured powders, especially crimson red, symbolising blessings and protection in Hindu culture.
[3] It refers to 'unbroken rice' and represents one of the preliminary rites in deity worship.
[4] It refers to the lit diyas (lamps) placed before deities during temple prayers, which are later used to bless worshippers.

COMRADE ANJANA

Bina Theeng Tamang

It had been almost nine years since I last saw Rohini. The last time was when I was on duty at the Dañdagauñ check post. After that, she disappeared. But now, unexpectedly, I saw her again at the very same army check post. She looked even more beautiful than I remembered, accompanied by a restless young boy, about seven years old. Seeing him, I was overwhelmed with a mix of emotions—a sense of emptiness and unease coursing through me. Despite all the years that had passed, I was struck by how little she had changed. Her appearance, complexion, and gait remained the same. Her fair skin, long hair, and blue eyes were just as they had been. The only noticeable difference was that her body had slightly broadened. Though she had gained a little weight, it only enhanced her beauty.

"When did you arrive, Rohini?" I began the conversation. She seemed startled, possibly because I had approached her so suddenly, or perhaps she hadn't recognised me. I had already noticed her earlier while she was making her way uphill, guiding her son.

"Oh my! Raju, is that you? You're stationed here?" Her surprise was evident.

"Yes, I've been here for two months now, after being transferred from the Nagarkot Barracks. And you? When did you get back to Nepal?" I asked, still amazed to see her after all these years.

"It's been about a month since I returned to Kathmandu. I've been staying in the city. Today, I was planning to visit my mother's place," she replied.

Noticing her weary expression, I figured she must have climbed that steep hill in about an hour. "Shyam, bring three chairs, please," I called out.

"Yes, sir," Shyam responded promptly, bringing the chairs from inside.

"Sit down, Rohini. You look exhausted," I said, noticing her weariness. "It seems your body isn't as cooperative as it used to be. You were so slender back then, leaping around like a young doe."

She let out a burst of laughter—one I hadn't heard in years. Her sweet, ringing laughter filled the air, and I found myself laughing along with her.

"Yes, Raju, my body is starting to give up on me now," she replied, still smiling. "Even this one-hour climb has worn me out. And my son kept insisting we rest every few steps."

"So, where's the boy's father?" I asked, curious about her husband. "And have you been wandering around here on your own?" I quickly tried to shift the conversation.

"Yes, this is the first time I've returned to Nepal since I fled. I came back because I really wanted to see my mother."

"That's good. One should never forget the mother who gave them life," I said, agreeing with her sentiment.

"True, but I won't stay in Nepal for long. I'll probably leave again in a few months," she added.

"Why? Don't you want to stay here?" The thought of her leaving again filled me with unease. She seemed saddened as well.

"What's there to stay for? Strikes, protests, corruption, and selfishness everywhere. We joined the war, hoping for change, but what did we really achieve? Life has to go on. Principles alone don't fill the stomach. To make a living, I'll have to return," she said, pouring out her disillusionment, frustration, and reality all at once.

I sensed her emotions—perhaps she was reminiscing about the past, especially the period of conflict. However, she seemed eager to continue, so she added, "We have an apple orchard in Kashmir. We work there, and it provides a decent income. We have enough to eat, wear, and even save a little."

Her face clearly reflected satisfaction. Though she once held a special place in my heart, she now belonged to someone else. Yet, she seemed genuinely happy, and her happiness brought me joy too, though it also weighed on my heart. Still, I kept my feelings to myself and remained silent.

She continued, "Did you get married?"

I felt a bit uncomfortable but replied, "Yes, I did. What else could I do? You were far away. I even have a little daughter now; she's two years old."

As I spoke, I noticed a faint trace of disquiet on her face. It seemed she was drifting back to memories of the times we spent together in school, in the same class.

We had studied together until the ninth grade, often arguing, but beneath those disputes was a hidden bond. Our relationship was intimate, and missing a day or skipping a quarrel made our routine feel incomplete. I enjoyed our playful fights; I would sit on the back bench, tug at her hair, and she would respond by hitting my hand with a ruler. That touch thrilled me, and I would whisper, "I love you," in her ear. She'd glare at me with her nose wrinkled in anger and her big eyes fierce, and I found a strange kind of love in that very gaze.

As classmates, we called each other names, which conveyed a sense of closeness. We were often together, whether doing chores or herding cattle. I would tease her, and she would chase me away with a cob of corn or a twig whip from the woods. But I was a boy; she could never catch me. Eventually, she would tire, and I would get moved by the sight of her sweat-soaked face. I would slow down so she could catch up, and once we met, she would gently stomp on my feet with hers, ensuring I wasn't too hurt. Only then would she feel fully satisfied. Perhaps this was where our love began to take root. Our arguments and quarrels only deepened our feelings. My boundless affection and her unspoken love played out in our struggles.

I roamed in a world of imagined love with her. In her gentle face, I saw my own reflection. I couldn't imagine a world without her. Our relationship was an open book, known to everyone—family, neighbours, friends, and acquaintances. The acceptance of all only strengthened our bond. We were confident that no one could sever the thread of our love. There were no obstacles in our way; our path was open, and we could walk it however we wished.

But our pure love seemed to be thwarted by fate, or perhaps cursed by some ill omen. An accidental mistake created a rift between us, as if acid had been poured over our happy world, causing us unbearable pain. This occurred around 1997, during the height of the Maoist insurgency. The Maoists were sparking rebellion from village to village, expanding their organisation by recruiting students in schools.

They came to our school too and included Rohini in their revolutionary student wing.

Thus, Rohini set out on this unforeseen path unknowingly. Despite my efforts to make her understand, she seemed under the sway of an unseen force and refused to listen. Soon, someone tipped off the police, who surrounded her house to arrest her. Her father managed to help her escape through the back window, and she fled to her aunt's house. But the police followed her there too. After a tense chase, she ended up connecting with her guerrilla comrades and, due to circumstances beyond her control, became an active Maoist cadre. She was given the underground name 'Anjana.' Although she wished otherwise, returning home was no longer an option, and the army's relentless raids in the village only fueled her commitment to the revolution.

Unaware of the true objectives of the Maoists, she spent nearly two years as a courier, delivering pamphlets and leaflets for the organisation. In this way, she became deeply involved in the Maoist movement, almost by accident. Meanwhile, I was in the village preparing for my SLC exams[1]. When Rohini came to take her exam, someone tipped off the authorities again, and security forces arrived immediately. The headmaster showed kindness and managed to help Rohini and her friends escape through the backdoor.

As a result, she was unable to continue her studies. Meanwhile, I felt like a fish impaled on a hook. I managed to pass my SLC exams, but then came the devastating news of my brother's death, which set our home ablaze with grief. My brother, serving as a soldier, had been killed in a Maoist ambush. The news left my family and me in shock. My sister-in-law's wailing and the children's cries fueled a burning

---

[1] School Leaving Certificate – In Nepal, Year 10 final exams were formerly known as SLC but are now called SEE (Secondary Education Examination).

desire for revenge within me. I felt an overwhelming urge to kill Maoists at the mere mention of their name. It was as if my brother's death had ignited a spark that was rapidly turning into a raging firestorm.

Determined to avenge my brother's death, I resolved to join the Nepal Army. At that time, many soldiers were leaving their jobs out of fear of the Maoists or due to pressure from their families, but I was consumed by a singular desire for revenge and ignored everyone's advice.

In the midst of this turmoil, even the warmth of our love began to chill. She, now an underground militant, and I, a soldier in the army, represented the clash of fire and water, making it seem impossible for our paths to converge. I lost all sense of calm. My posting was at Singhadurbar—the seat of the Nepal government—while Rohini had become a true Maoist insurgent with the nom de guerre 'Anjana.' We had become like two opposing banks of a river, perhaps caught in the game of fate.

The following year, after finally being granted leave, I went home for Dashain. By then, I had given up hope of ever seeing Rohini again. Each time I confronted the reality of her being a Maoist, it erupted into a storm of anger and hatred. I had made up my mind to distance myself from her, someone who once meant so much to me. With the situation being unfavourable for returning home during the conflict, I invited my parents to meet me at the district headquarters.

The day I arrived at the district headquarters was one of the harshest and most painful of my life. Thirteen or fourteen soldiers from Nepal Army paraded through town, draping the muzzle of their guns with women's clothing and chanting loudly, "Anjana is dead today." For a moment, it felt like a bad dream, but it was a harsh reality. I was horrified, as though night had fallen in broad daylight. The soldiers were indeed carrying Rohini's belongings—her bag, clothes, and slippers.

I should have felt vindicated, knowing that one of my brother's murderers was dead. But my heart was not at peace. Instead, it ached even more. The pain was so overwhelming that it was almost unbearable. The news of her death left me devastated, as if the earth spiraled into chaos.

I broke down into bitter tears and cried alone in the room, overcome by grief. With Rohini's death, I felt as though I was dying bit by bit. The world seemed alien, and life appeared meaningless. Perhaps it was the profound love I had for her spilling out relentlessly through my tears. The pull of our opposing poles still lingered. Her death had painted my life entirely in shades of sorrow—colours that neither faded nor could be erased. It felt like the culmination of our selfless love.

There was a time when I didn't even want to hear her name. I thought she was stubborn and ignored my advice. I believed I had killed the love I once felt for her, convinced that I hated her rather than loved her. But that was all false and delusional; otherwise, I wouldn't have felt such intense pain that day. The memory of Rohini tormented me constantly. I lived as though I were perpetually dying. I lost all attachment to life, firing recklessly even in intense confrontations. I had no regard for my own safety, yet somehow, I always survived.

About seven months later, I was posted to Dañdagauñ, tasked with inspecting public vehicles entering and exiting Nuwakot. As usual, we began checking vehicles early in the morning. One such vehicle, heading from Nuwakot to Kathmandu, stopped at the checkpoint. We asked everyone to disembark. As people hurriedly stepped out, I went inside the vehicle alone to ensure no one was left behind. In that moment, I thought I sensed some movement on the back seat. The bus was dark inside, and shadows seemed to shift. A thrill of sensation coursed through me as suspicion grew. But then, it fell quiet again, and I felt a sense of relief.

Now curiosity got the best of me. I had to find out what was really happening. Slowly, I moved forward, and there I saw a woman lying curled up on the seat, her entire body wrapped in a shawl. I gently pulled the shawl back, my heart trembling with an unknown fear. To my surprise, it was Rohini lying there. My hands began to shake. It seemed like months had passed since she last combed her hair. Her face, pale and almost colourless, showed signs of weakness. Despite her frail condition, the sight of Rohini alive—someone I had thought was dead—filled me with indescribable joy. For a moment, it felt like a dream. I pinched myself to make sure it was real. It indeed was.

Yet, finding her in such a state also filled me with distress. I grew restless, caught between conflicting emotions, unsure of what to do. She seemed to recognise me and stared at me closely. Just then, a voice snapped me out of my thoughts, "Is anyone left inside?"

"No, sir," I replied instinctively. For the first time, I failed in my duty. I knew that if they found Rohini, they wouldn't spare her. Somehow, I was protecting my adversary. I didn't want Rohini to die—I wanted her to live. At that moment, lying didn't feel wrong at all. I looked deeply into her eyes. She looked terribly weak, maybe she hadn't had any food or water for days. From the depths of my heart, a boundless love emerged. I wanted to embrace her and cry out loud, but I was helpless. Duty shackled my hands. Even though I desperately wanted to express the love and care I still felt for her, I couldn't.

She must have recognised me too, for she glanced at me briefly before lowering her head. No words were exchanged between us—only our eyes spoke. She seemed grateful for the compassion I had shown, as she cast a tender look in my direction.

I stepped off the bus, burdened with a heavy heart. Moments later, the bus sped off toward its destination, leaving me standing there, speechless. As the bus moved farther away, it felt as if someone had torn my heart out and taken it along. I wanted to run after the bus, but an intense ache settled in my chest, holding me back. Helpless, I had no choice but to remain standing where I was.

The next day, I forcefully took leave from work, claiming that I needed to take my mother to Kathmandu for treatment. The truth was, I had a feeling that Rohini might be staying at her younger aunt's house, so I went straight there. Sure enough, Rohini was there. Overcome with joy, my heart soared into the blue skies. It felt as though a few drops of water had finally fallen on a withering plant.

She was lying on the bed. As soon as she saw me, she smiled faintly and gestured for me to sit close. There was a strange pleasure in being near her again. She adjusted her pillow slightly higher and leaned against the wall. In my heart, I wished she could lean against me instead, that I could hold her in my arms. But fear held me back, and I quickly calmed myself.

"I never imagined, not even in the slightest, that I would see you again," I said. "I was devastated by the news of your death."

She threw a faint smile, drained of any colour, and began to speak. "Honestly, I never thought I would see you again in this lifetime either. But fate was strong. If you hadn't been there yesterday, I wouldn't be here today. I owe you countless thanks."

It was that "thank you" that stung me the most. To ease the

sting, I replied, "Why are you saying this? I let you go because I loved you. If it had been someone else in your place, I wouldn't have let them go. But there was something magical about you; my hands just couldn't move."

I was eager to uncover who had spread the false news of her death, so I gently probed into the mystery. Rohini took a deep breath and, with a voice heavy with the weight of past, began to share her story—

"That day, I missed my mother terribly. Without telling anyone, I ran away to the district headquarters. I had heard that my mother was coming to my uncle's house. Someone must have tipped them off because the police were already there, waiting in full force even before I arrived. I was unarmed and completely vulnerable.

Since it was the district headquarters, they had influence. We rarely went there during the day, and for good reason. They had been roaming around with my photo, looking for me. As I approached my uncle's house, I sensed something was off—an eerie tension, a smell of enemy scheming. My eyes grew suspicious. I had this premonition that something unpleasant was about to happen. The usual hustle and bustle of the headquarters was gone. The shops were closed. It hit me like a jolt—was this a preparation for some kind of battle?

My suspicions were correct. Before I even had time to think, they started firing at me. I used some of the combat skills I had learned in the company of my comrades. Dodging bullets wasn't easy, but somehow, I managed to evade the barrage of gunfire and escape into the forest. Once I was in the forest, running became difficult, so I pulled out a tracksuit from my bag and changed into it, along with my combat shoes. I left my slippers and kurta behind and fled as fast as I could. Bullets whizzed by—some near my shoulder, others under my legs.

Death seemed to be closing in on me, with monstrous, grotesque figures chasing after me. As I ran through the jungle, thorny bushes and stinging nettles clawed at my body, leaving me bloodied. Despite the pain, I refused to give up. It was a relentless game of cat and mouse between the police and me. My trail was marked with drops of blood, and as I fled, I reached a large cliff with no way forward. The thought of jumping into the chasm seemed less daunting than falling into the hands of enemies and facing a life of torment. With no other options, I took the leap.

By some twist of fate, or perhaps because my time had not yet come, I survived the plunge into the waterfall below. I found myself sprawled on the other side of the ravine, barely able to breathe. For a moment, I lay face down, unable to move. Believing that no one could have survived such a fall, my enemies assumed I was dead. They took my clothes and slippers and left, shouting "Anjana is dead today," their voices echoing triumphantly through the jungle. I felt a wave of relief, knowing they would no longer search for me.

I dragged my injured body slowly, making my way to Kaulé as the day drew to a close. Exhausted, I collapsed into unconsciousness. The next day, a village woman discovered me hidden under a stack of straw. She took me to her home and nursed me back to health. It took two days for me to regain consciousness, after which she told me everything that had happened.

For months, I lived in the village, doing odd jobs like carrying manure and breaking clods of earth, but my health continued to deteriorate. Everyone urged me to seek treatment in Kathmandu, so I left just yesterday. Had I been able to walk, I would have taken the jungle route, but my body wouldn't cooperate, so I had to travel by bus. If it weren't for you, they would have caught me yesterday. Once again, thank you so much."

Rohini recounted the entire ordeal in one breath, and it felt like I was witnessing a scene from a harrowing movie. Rohini seemed like a real-life hero, victorious in the end, and I felt a deep sense of pride in being part of her courageous journey.

Her treatment in Kathmandu couldn't continue due to the constant threat of raids and the risk of being discovered by the army. Following her aunt's advice, arrangements were made for her to go to Kashmir in India, where her elder aunt lived. The separation was painful, but for her safety, I had to endure it in silence. The next day, as I waved goodbye, my heart shuddered as if caught in a powerful quake.

After that, we never met again. I would occasionally visit her aunt's house to inquire about Rohini's well-being. Two years after she had moved to Kashmir, I learned that she had married a Nepali man from the area, following her aunt's advice, as staying there would have burdened the family further. My heart, once so entwined with hers, now belonged to someone else. In this game of love, I lost completely.

Today, the same Rohini stood before me, content and satisfied with her life. Though I could no longer have her, I was happy for her. My only wish now was for her to stay. With the conflict over and former insurgents living freely, there was no longer any danger. I said, "You can stay here now."

I waited for a positive response, but there was no sign of enthusiasm or attachment to my suggestion. Ignoring my request, she said, "I sacrificed my life for the hope of change and devoted myself to the revolution. I made a significant sacrifice, but nothing has turned out as we hoped. Those we fought for remain as poor as ever, while the wealthy grow even wealthier. The leaders of the revolution have seen dramatic improvements in their own lives, but the change we ordinary people expected seems elusive. Just forget about it! I don't want to think about revolution or change anymore. I will not stay in Nepal. One must keep rolling with life wherever it takes you and somehow make do. I am fed up with this meaningless change."

Her words left me astonished. Rohini, who once spoke fervently about change and revolution, now seemed profoundly disillusioned. It was distressing to see her in such a state.

As evening approached, she was eager to climb the hill and reach her mother's place before nightfall. I bade her farewell as she began her ascent. Watching her slowly climb the steep path, I reflected on her transformation and the state of affairs. Had the change the Nepali people longed for truly arrived? Was the country living up to the dreams of the martyrs? In villages, old women still use traditional millstones by the dim light of wick lamps, and villagers risk their lives crossing rivers on precarious wire bridges. Nepalese continue to shed their blood on foreign lands and burn in hot deserts. Whether Maoist militants, army personnel, or ordinary citizens, all who sacrificed their lives were children of Mother Nepal. What has the 12-year people's war really changed? I continued to ponder these questions. ◆

Drama

THE BULL

Bhimnidhi Tiwari

PROLOGUE:

King Rana Bahadur Shah had a deep passion for raising four-legged livestock, particularly bulls. He started the tradition of branding a bull with hot iron and releasing it every month at the Pashupatinath Temple. He also managed the vast cow pasture known as Thulo Gauchar, where an airport stands now. Among the many bulls he raised, one named 'Maalé' fell ill. The king had warned the bull doctor, "You'll be punished if you bring news of the bull's death." But the bull died. This one-act play dramatises the events that followed.

—Playwright

CHARACTERS:

• **Rana Bahadur Shah:** The 23-year-old king.
• **Laxmi Narayan Dahal (Jaisi):** A 40-year-old *Subedār*[1] with Samarjung Company, *Ditthā*[2] at the ItaChapali court, and a traditional bull doctor.

---

[1] A military rank roughly equivalent to that of a warrant officer.
[2] A legal or administrative officer in a local court.

- **Jitman:** A cowherd.
- **Goré:** Another cowherd.

Scene I

Location: Yard

Time: Dawn

Month: Ashwin (B.S.[3] 1854)

[Birds chirp in the trees as the red sun casts its glow over the yard and onto Laxmi Narayan, who is seated on the carpet in a squatting position.]

Laxmi Narayan: *(Looking backstage)* How reckless and wild you all are, like an untethered bull! Even with seven wives, I find no peace. I'm waiting for a drag of hookah, but no one bothers to bring it. *(Shouting)* Hey, Nepti! Chyanti! Putali! Gauthali! Thuli! Ghormukha! May you all meet your end at once! You all pretend not to hear, though I know you do. Everywhere I turn, it's just rivalry and discontent.

[Jitman and Goré rush in, panting heavily.]

Laxmi Narayan: What's going on? How is the bull?

Goré: *(Bowing his head in reverence)* He's dead, sir. The bull is dead.

Laxmi Narayan: *(Startled)* What?

Jitman: *(Bowing his head)* He's just passed away.

Laxmi Narayan: He's really dead?

Jitman: His body is stiff, and his eyes are lifeless.

Goré: His tail has gone limp.

Laxmi Narayan: Now your father will punish us. He'll have me

---

[3] An acronym of Bikram Sambat—the official Nepali calendar. It is a lunar-solar calendar that typically runs 57 years ahead of the Gregorian calendar.

shaved, and you both will be beheaded. We're finished!

Jitman: *(Panicking)* What should we do, sir? Should I flee to my home in Dhunibesi? I can't leave my younger son behind.

Goré: *(Panicking)* What should we do, sir? You need to save us. Life is precious.

Laxmi Narayan: How can you hope to save yourselves? He once had my mouth burned for speaking too loudly. *(Points to his mouth)* See the black burn mark? I still can't grow a moustache on this side. And now, with the bull dead, how will we save ourselves? *(Reflects for a moment)* But wait. I'll do my best to protect you both. But how will I save myself? How did that young bull die?

Goré: It's not wise to talk big with a small mouth. But how can a beast that lives on grass digest fine rice and lentil soup? Prices have soared just because of this. A *pāthi*⁴ of rice now costs a rupee, and a *dhārni*⁵ of ghee is nearly three-quarters of a rupee. Ordinary people can't even afford basic cornmeal, but this animal feasts on guavas, bananas, and sugarcanes every day, not just once or twice a week.

Jitman: That's true. We sleep on straw beds in winter, while the bull enjoys a mattress, quilt, and mosquito net. Oh, the injustice!

Laxmi Narayan: You're right. Go stay in the cowshed. Don't let anyone find out the bull is dead. Act as if you're taking care of it, just like usual. I'll head to the palace now. I have many enemies, and if word gets out before I reach, there'll be no hope for us. Now go! *(Calling to the backstage)* Hey, Khatri! Get the horse ready.

[The cowherds exit. One of the wives enters, carrying a hookah

---

⁴ One pāthi is about 4.5 to 5 kg, used for measuring grains in Nepal.
⁵ A traditional unit of weight in Nepal, one dhārni is roughly equivalent to 2.5 kg.

and pipe.]

Laxmi Narayan: I'm on the verge of losing everything. My head is about to be shaved in punishment. How can you expect me to enjoy a hookah now? *(Scolding)* Take it away!

[He exits. The wife stands there, bewildered and confused.]

Scene II

Location: Courtyard of Basantapur Palace

Time/Month: Same (Later from the previous scene)

[Laxmi Narayan arrives and stands reverently, gazing up towards the window.]

Rana Bahadur: *(Commandingly from backstage)* What's the matter?

Laxmi Narayan: *(Bowing deeply)* Greetings, Your Majesty! Long live Your Majesty!

Rana Bahadur: Why have you come here so early, Dahal? Tell me Lachhé, what's going on?

Laxmi Narayan: *(Joining hands in a polite gesture)* Your Majesty, I must seek your favour regarding a pressing issue. I fear what might happen if I don't ask for your help. But, even making this request brings me unbearable anguish. The bull— I'm not sure what's happened. The sun is already high, and he hasn't woken up. We served him his meal, but he didn't eat. He remains still and silent, lying as if in a deep slumber.

Rana Bahadur: What? Are you saying he's dead?

Laxmi Narayan: His eyes are fixed and lifeless.

Rana Bahadur: Wait, I'll come down right now.

Laxmi Narayan: *(Wiping sweat from his forehead and taking a* *deep breath)* Oh Ram! Oh Krishna!

[After a moment]

[Laxmi Narayan remains in a reverent stance. Rana Bahadur enters.]

Rana Bahadur: So, what's the verdict? Is he dead or not?

Laxmi Narayan: He hasn't passed away yet.

Rana Bahadur: What do you have to say then?

Laxmi Narayan: Your Majesty, just as not all humans are alike, so too are not all bulls. You are a revered leader, celebrated far and wide, while I am but a lowly Brahmin. Similarly, Maalé, with his strong build, grace, and valor, is unmatched. No other bull compares to him. I am deeply concerned about his health. Should I move him to the hill for a change in weather before it gets too hot here? Rest is Your Majesty's order.

Rana Bahadur: Very well. Take him immediately. Do you need any soldiers to assist you?

Laxmi Narayan: The cowherds will be more helpful than soldiers. They understand his needs and know how to make him comfortable.

Rana Bahadur: Go ahead. You should accompany them as well.

Laxmi Narayan: Your Majesty, this Brahmin must also go. I need to check his pulse and administer medicine regularly. May I take my leave now?

Rana Bahadur: Yes, go. Make sure he is taken away with utmost care.

Laxmi Narayan: *(Cheerfully)* Long live Your Majesty! Cheers to Your Majesty!

[As Rana Bahadur goes inside, Laxmi Narayan exits.]

Rana Bahadur: *(Re-entering)* Dahal! Dahal! Dahal! Lachhé! Look here! Listen!

Laxmi: *(Entering)* Your Majesty!

Rana Bahadur: I will go see him right away. If he gets better here, why take him to the hill? There's no need to trouble him unnecessarily.

Laxmi: *(Bowing with joined hands)* The medicine here has provided some relief but hasn't cured him entirely. Perhaps, a change in weather might help.

Rana Bahadur: I'll see him myself. *(Looking backstage)* We'll take a royal convoy. Get the palanquin ready. Dahal, understood? We're going together. Wait for me outside the door.

Laxmi: Yes, Your Majesty!

[Both exit.]

Scene III

Location: A cowshed at Thulo Gauchar

Time: Morning

Month: Same

[The bull lies dead on a thick mattress. Jitman and Goré sit in a squatting position around it.]

Jitman: We were two brothers until today, but now we're going to be four.

Goré: Do you really think he'll behead us?

Jitman: What makes you think we'll survive?

Goré: Dahal Sir has gone to see the king. Let's see what news he brings.

Jitman: He's a cunning man. He has the king's ear. He'll find a way to save himself. It's us who will be victims. We'd better escape.

Goré: Where can the sheep of the pen escape? They'll bring us back and behead us anyway. *(Looking afar)* Look, Jité! The king seems to be on his way.

Jitman: *(Staring in that direction)* Yes, the palanquin in front, and Dahal Sir following on foot. After him, Khatri is walking the horse.

Goré: What do we do? We're surely going to be killed today.

Jitman: This cursed bull! He died, and now he's taking us with him.

Goré: Look, the palanquin has stopped. The convoy is in the meadow. *(Panicking)* Look, look! How fast they're approaching! Dahal Sir is running towards us, ahead of the others.

Jitman: What does he have to say now?

Laxmi Narayan: *(Entering hurriedly)* Jité, massage the hind feet. You, Goré, fan him from the front. Bow down and don't dare look up. Don't say a word about the bull being dead. Get moving, quick! There's no guarantee whether you'll live or die today.

[Jitman starts massaging the bull's hind legs. Goré begins fanning from the front. Nearby, in a mortar, Laxmi Narayan quickly grinds medicine.]

Rana Bahadur: *(Entering, in a commanding voice)* Maalé! Eh, Maalé! What happened to you? Get up! Get up!

Laxmi Narayan: Since midnight, Your Majesty—till now, *(Pointing towards Jitman)* he's been massaging the feet. *(Pointing towards Goré)* He's been fanning continuously. I've been preparing and administering medicine all the while. The bull swallows the medicine without hesitation. But he neither gets up nor moves. He doesn't bellow, and he won't eat. He just listens and stares blankly.

Rana Bahadur: Huh? What happened to him? Maalé? Get up! Are there any fruits? Bring them, Dahal!

[Laxmi Narayan goes out and immediately returns with a hand of bananas.]

Laxmi Narayan: Here are bananas, Your Majesty!

Rana Bahadur: *(Extending bananas to the bull's mouth)* Eat, Maalé! Have some! Dahal, what's wrong with him? He doesn't breathe or eat. Seems he's dead.

Laxmi Narayan: But he looks well with his eyes open.

Rana Bahadur: Look, his ears are drooping, his tail is loose. He's dead. What change of weather could help him now? He has already died.

[Upon hearing that the bull is dead, Jitman starts crying, placing his head on the bull's thigh. Seeing this, Goré stops fanning and falls on the bull's horns, also crying.]

Jitman: *(Crying)* I took care of you from your childhood. I brushed you and massaged your feet. Today, you've left me an orphan, Sir Bull. Where have you gone? *(Looking at Rana Bahadur, beating his chest)* Your Majesty! What should I do now? I am burning with pain inside.

Rana Bahadur: Hey cowherd! Why do you cry? He's simply dead. What can we do about that?

Jitman: My heart won't accept it, Your Majesty! No, it won't. My Maalé! What should I do? What fate is this?

Rana Bahadur: Hey Dahal! Console him.

Laxmi Narayan: How can he accept it? How can he be consoled? He is deeply hurt.

Rana Bahadur: Don't cry. You'll receive a reward of four hundred rupees. Keep quiet now.

[Hearing that Jitman received a reward of four hundred rupees, Goré also starts sobbing and falls at the bull's feet.]

Goré: For your sake, I didn't think of anything else—home, mother, father, wife, or children. Sir Bull, I will go with you. Either I'll hang myself or be buried with you. I can't leave you. *(Beating his chest)* No, I can't.

Rana Bahadur: Hey, Dahal. Console him too.

Laxmi Narayan: Don't worry, Goré. You'll also receive a favour from His Highness. He's suffered greatly, Your Majesty. He wouldn't let a single fly sit on the bull's body. He would fan him day and night, taking care of him constantly. Every morning, he'd bow to all four feet of the bull, calling him 'father.' He's now an orphan, a helpless one.

Goré: *(Crying inconsolably)* Your Majesty! What should I do? I should have died instead of him.

Rana Bahadur: Keep quiet. You'll also receive a reward of five hundred rupees. Stop crying now.

Laxmi Narayan: *(Acting as if the agony is coming from deep inside, in a choked voice)* For the sake of the bull, I too didn't think of hunger, thirst, or sleep. I compromised my service to Your Majesty to care for him day and night. If he were alive today, I can't imagine the rewards I'd receive! But now, my own fate seems broken. I administered all kinds of syrups and medicines. His body grew strong and healthy. At such a young age, he became a valiant fighter, defeating other bulls. And now, in his prime, right in front of my eyes... *(Failing to control* *himself, he sobs.)*

Rana Bahadur: *(Berating)* A *Subedār* of the company and a *Ditthā*, and still crying like a child. Why? Can't you soothe yourself? Quiet now! *(Leaving)* Bury him with your own hands. Perform the funeral rites. Make all the donations and offerings for yourself. I'll take care of your needs.

[Rana Bahadur exits. Laxmi Narayan follows him.]

[After a while]

Jitman: Oh God! We survived. *(Wiping sweat with his cap)* This piece of junk almost got us killed!

Goré: *(Fanning himself, taking a deep breath)* I thought I was finished today. Thank God, we survived!

(THE CURTAIN FALLS) ◆

IN QUEST OF SPRING

Ashesh Malla

[A wide-open street. On one side, an old man sits in deep meditation. The Narrator rushes toward the audience, appearing frantic.]

Narrator: *(Grabbing an audience member)* Have you seen my dove? Where could it have gone? Please, tell me—haven't you seen it? Who took my dove? *(Desperately scans the audience, then dashes away.)*

My dove's wings have been clipped; it can't fly. Who would steal my poor dove? *(Sighs)* Alright, I'll be honest—I'm actually here to perform a play. And yes, I had a dove with me too. So after the play, if you happen to find it, please return my dove to me...

Now, let's get on with it! The play begins! But, truth be told, this play actually started a long, long time ago. It had already begun when I was just a child. My grandmother used to tell me—'Dear, this play had already started when I was young.'

But today—today, I'll bring this play to an end.

Oh, you must be wondering who I am. Me? I'm the narrator of this play. But why do you even need my introduction? Look over there, see that old man? He's been meditating in this very spot for hundreds of years.

(Pointing to the air) Hey, look at that old tree! Just like this old man, this tree has a history. When you think of a tree, you might picture green leaves and birds nesting in its branches. But this tree—look at it, it's all withered and decrepit. There are no leaves, and the branches are rotting and about to fall. The leaves have all dried up... Do you know why it hasn't grown any new leaves? Because Spring hasn't come. Without Spring, it can't be green. Spring is nowhere to be found—why doesn't it come?

See, this old man has been meditating here for years, trying to bring that very Spring into existence. His chest is full of holes from termites, just like this old tree.

If we find Spring today, this play will come to an end. I'll do my best to make that happen...

[The narrator moves toward the audience. Suddenly, a voice shouting "Spring!" echoes from a distance. A person rushes through the audience and grabs the narrator.]

Person: *(Rejoicing)* Spring! My Spring! Where have you been? Why did you run away from me? Where did you go, Spring?

Narrator: Are you out of your mind? Who's Spring? I'm not Spring or anything like that. My name is Himalaya Prasad...

Person: Himalaya? If you're Himalaya, then where's the snow on your head?

Narrator: What nonsense! Just because my name is Himalaya doesn't mean there's snow on my head, got it? There are names like 'Wrestler' here, but they get blown away with a gentle breeze. There are fools known by wise names. Here, the name is one thing, but the reality is quite the opposite, understand?

Person: If you weren't Spring, you could've just said so! Was a long lecture really necessary?

Narrator: Giving lectures is my forte.

Person: You mentioned Spring earlier. You must know where it is. Tell me, where is it?

[The narrator pauses thoughtfully.]

Narrator: Are you searching for the same Spring?

Person: Which Spring? Yes... I am searching for Spring. My Spring...

Narrator: Spring? Look at this old man here, who has been meditating for years to find Spring. You won't find Spring by shouting in the streets, mister. You need to meditate, just like this old man...

[The narrator starts walking down the street.]

Person: Baba! Have you also been searching for Spring? Baba! Please tell me, where is Spring? Why aren't you speaking, Baba? *(To the audience)* Who has stolen Baba's voice? Who has stolen Baba's sight? Who has taken Baba's...! Baba! Why are you silent? Fine, you won't speak? I'll search for it myself, I'll search for it myself... Spring!

[He tries to run down another street, shouting. A boy rushes towards him from that direction. The boy's entire body is burnt, and he stands in front of the person, groaning in pain. The person looks at him in shock.]

Boy: *(Blocking the person's way)* Brother, don't go there. Don't go there.

Person: Why not?

Boy: *(Blowing on his burnt hands)* Ouch, it burns, it burns! Brother, don't go there.

Person: *(Irritated)* Why? Why shouldn't I go?

Boy: There's a fire over there. Fire...

Person: Fire? Where? Where is the fire?

Boy: On the street.

Person: On the street?

Boy: *(Wincing in pain)* Yes, brother, the street is on fire. The stones and soil are burning fiercely. Look at my hands—they're all burnt.

Person: How did the stones and soil catch fire?

Boy: I don't know how! A lot of people were coming, and as they approached, the street caught fire. The stones and soil just started burning. Some people got burnt and died on the spot, while others ran away. Some broke their hands, some burned their feet...

Person: Where were those people going?

Boy: We were all searching for Spring, brother!

Person: Searching for Spring?

Boy: I'm not going anymore. I won't search for Spring again, even if it means my death. It hurts too much...

Person: What's your connection to Spring?

Boy: I don't know; I've never met it.

Person: Then why did you go searching?

Boy: What could I do when everyone else was going? So, I went along too. But now, I won't go anymore. Look, I burned my hands for nothing.

[The boy leaves, blowing on his hands. A young man enters.]

Person: Excuse me...

[The young man glances at him.]

Person: Where are you coming from?

Young Man: Huh? Why?

Person: They say there's a fire on the street over there!

Young Man: *(Laughing)* Fire? On the streets? Are you out of your mind?

Person: I'm not crazy. There's a fire on the street over there!

Young Man: Don't be ridiculous. There's no fire. And even if there were, there are plenty of fire trucks and water. What are you talking about? I just came from that street, and there's no fire at all.

Person: Did you see Spring there?

Young Man: Spring? What are you talking about?

Person: My...

Young Man: *(Interrupting)* Your what? I don't even know you. It's not right to bother someone who's just passing by.

Person: Who's bothering you? If you're in a hurry, just go! All I asked was, "Did you see Spring?"

Young Man: *(Leaving)* Speak more politely. *(Pauses and turns back as if remembering something)* Oh, never mind... *(Exits)*

[One of the audience members stands up.]

Audience Member 1: Why is everyone silent? Why are you just sitting there? There's a fire over there, and people are getting burned! And yet, you're all just watching!

Audience Member 2: Hey, who are you to tell us what to do? We're here to watch the play. If there's a fire and people get burned, that's not our problem.

Audience Member 1: Coward! Selfish!

Audience Member 2: Watch your language! Don't insult the audience who's here to enjoy the play.

Audience Member 1: Fine... I'm going. I'll go put out the fire myself... *(Leaves.)*

[A madman enters, holding a stone. The audience member sits back down.]

Madman: *(Holding a stone)* Maybe I should just smash your skull! Why did you steal my heart? Should I kill you? Should I hit you with this stone? *(Looks at the old man under the tree)* Who are you? Vishwamitra, or someone else? Why are you sitting here meditating? Speak up! Do you want a boon? The ages of getting boons through penance are over. Get up, grab a stone, and come with me.

[He shakes the old man, but the old man remains motionless. He nudges and tickles him, but the old man doesn't respond.]

Didn't you hear me? Hey, Vishwamitra[1]! Do you need Menaka[2] to wake you up? *(Shouts)* Get up, Vishwamitra, get up! Stop meditating like this! Penance won't get you anything. You need to take a stone and march.

[A gardener enters, holding wilted plants.]

Gardener: *(Singing)* Spring never arrived.

Madman: Who are you?

Gardener: Me? I'm a gardener.

Madman: What do you want?

Gardener: Flowers, of course! I want flowers, what else? Haven't you noticed no flowers have bloomed? Look at this. The plants are dried up and dead; no flowers have bloomed.

Madman: Flowers will bloom, why wouldn't they?

---

[1] A revered sage in Hindu mythology, he pleased the gods with his intense meditation.
[2] A celestial nymph sent by the gods to distract Vishwamitra from his meditation.

Gardener: The flowers didn't bloom. At the crossroads on the hill, there's an old woman who waits every evening for her son to return, holding a withered flower in her hand. Did you know that?

Madman: A withered flower?

Gardener: Yes, she waits there with a withered flower *(laughs)*, but her son is already dead. She doesn't know. *(Singing as he leaves)* Spring never arrived.

[The person from earlier comes running in.]

Person: Ouch! It burns, it burns!

Madman: Where? What happened?

Person: The street over there is on fire. My whole body is burned, it hurts...

Madman: Then why did you walk on a burning street?

Person: I was searching for Spring, but I couldn't find it.

Madman: You'll find it at the poultry farm. I'll bring it back.

Person: *(Excited)* At the poultry farm?

Madman: Yes. It eats, sleeps, wakes up in the morning, and crows.

Person: That's nonsense. A poultry farm has chickens, not Spring.

[Suddenly, the old man under the tree opens his eyes and starts coughing.]

Person: You're awake?

Madman: *(Spitting)* This one's mad—a fool. He must think he's a hero for doing penance. I carry a stone around; someday, I'll bash him with it.

Person: Hey! Don't insult him. He's been doing penance to find Spring. Do you understand?

Madman: *(Laughing)* Don't talk about Spring or any of that nonsense; no one finds it through penance. You need to throw stones. Whoever took it, you should smash their skull with a stone.

Old Man: *(Rising with a slight smile)* You're still a child. Drop the stone. Stones achieve nothing. Learn the lesson of peace. Learn to work. Don't panic. You must practise penance, true penance.

Person: Yes, you must practise penance.

Madman: *(Shouting)* Penance, huh? Rust yourself with penance, is that what you want? You keep to your penance and nonsense... I'll bring back Spring with this stone!

[Shouting, he exits.]

Old Man: *(Patting the person)* You're searching for Spring too, aren't you? Then come, walk with me. Let's go!

Person: There's a fire over there; it's raging.

Old Man: Fire and water are life, my child! To find Spring, you must walk through fire and get drenched by water... Finding what's lost isn't easy... Come... Come... Let's walk through the fire and begin our quest for Spring...

[They both exit. The narrator enters.]

Narrator: What a tragic play this is! Even today, it didn't end. I thought I'd finish it, but Spring is still not found... Until Spring is found, this play will continue. Come, let's end this play, come, let's search for Spring, come...

[The narrator invites the audience to follow, and some begin to follow him.] ◆

Essay

TIBET, MADHESH AND NEPAL

Baburam Acharya

The purpose of this essay is not to provide a detailed description of Tibet, Madhesh, and Nepal, but rather to explore the origins, meanings, and implications of these terms.

First, let's examine the term *Tibet*. Tibet is a high plateau, situated between fourteen and fifteen thousand feet above sea level, and bordered by the Kunlun Mountains to the north and the Himalayan ranges to the south. This region is known for its distinctive natural features and its unique linguistic and cultural identity. Since the time of Genghis Khan in the 13th century, Tibet has had political connections with the Chinese mainland, either directly or indirectly.

From what we know of history, Tibet remained relatively primitive until the early 6th century. It was during the mid-sixth century that signs of civilisation began to emerge, leading to the formation of the first organised state. The second ruler of this state, Songtsen Gampo (circa 570–650 AD), gained significant power. He opened previously inaccessible mountain passes in Yunnan (now called *Kuti*) and Kyirong, which facilitated travel to Nepal. Additionally, he sent emissaries to

Nepal to acquire scripts, which he used to develop his own writing system. He also embraced Nepali artistic skills and founded the city of Lhasa, meaning 'Land of the Gods.'

The people of this region originally referred to their land and themselves as *Bod*, although they wrote it as *Pot*. This convention is still used today. Due to local pronunciation differences, Nepalese began calling this region *Bhotta*, a term that remained once popular in Nepal. Over time, *Bhotta* evolved into *Bhot*, which is now commonly used in everyday speech.

However, the Mongol people to the north, for some reason, added the prefix *Ti* to *Bod* or *Pot* resulting in *Tibot* or *Tipot*. When this term reached Europe, it was pronounced as *Tibet* in accordance with Teutonic pronunciation. In Iran, *Tibet* became *Tibbat* according to Persian pronunciation, which has influenced the use of *Tibbat* in Urdu and other Indian languages. As the term *Tibbat* or *Tibet* gained international recognition, the inhabitants of the region also began using *Tibet* to refer to their country. Nonetheless, in national contexts, it is appropriate to use the traditional term *Bhot*, while *Tibet* or *Tibbat* should be used in international contexts.

However, earlier officials with limited knowledge sometimes misused the term *Bhot*. For example, terms like *Bhot Namlang* and *Chharka Bhot* are often cited incorrectly. North of the well-known *Lama Bagar* on the banks of the Tamakoshi River, there is a village named *Namlang*, inhabited by Sherpas, located on the border with Tibet. Although Sherpas practice Buddhism, their language and culture differ significantly from those of Tibetans. Tibetan culture includes practices such as multiple brothers marrying the same woman, which is absent among Sherpas. Therefore, Sherpas should not be classified as Tibetans. Referring to the Sherpa village of

Namlang in Nepal as *Bhot Namlang* in official documents and census reports is inaccurate.

In the eastern part of Jumla, there are two well-known settlements called *Chharka* and *Tarap* in the Himalayan region. The inhabitants of these settlements, much like the Sherpas, seem to come from families of southern origins. Their language and culture also do not resemble Tibetan traditions. Unlike the Sherpas, there is no evidence that they adopted Buddhism from Tibet. In this context, they appear entirely Nepalese. Despite this, official documents, census reports, and even maps of Nepal label the area as *Chharka Bhot*, which misleadingly suggests that this region is part of Tibet. Such inaccuracies can hinder national development. It is crucial for experts to address this issue with care.

In ancient times, the northern plains of India were divided into two regions: *Udīchya* (northern) and *Prāchya* (eastern). Due to differences in the languages of these regions, the grammarian Pāṇini of the 6th century BCE noted this linguistic division. Sanskrit grammarians recognised the Śarāvatī River as the boundary line between these two regions. The renowned lexicographer of the 4th century, Amarsingh, also cited the Śarāvatī River as the dividing line between *Udīchya* and the higher regions. However, the exact location of this river is now unknown. In modern times, some speculate that the Saraswati River, which lies between Uttar Pradesh and Punjab, might be another name for the Śarāvatī. However, Amarsingh also separately mentions a river named Saraswati.

According to these divisions, the plains of the Sindhu-Sutlej rivers were part of *Udīchya*, while the plains of the Ganga River fell under *Prāchya*. In ancient times, the regions corresponding to present-day Uttar Pradesh, Bihar, Odisha, Bengal, and Assam were considered part of *Prāchya*. In the 6th century BCE, Lord Gautam Buddha spread Buddhism in Awadh and Bihar. Later, during the Shunga era, orthodox Brahmins in the Ganga and Yamuna plains resisted Buddhism and reclassified the Awadh region from *Udīchya* to *Prāchya*. They renamed the plains from Ambala to Prayag as *Madhyadesh*. As a result, the *Manusmriti* described this region as holy land, viewing regions where Buddhism prevailed as impure.

The term *Madhyadesh* appears to have been influenced by Buddhist practice. Gautam Buddha advocated the Middle Path (*Madhyam Marg*), and thus the region where Buddhism flourished—Awadh and Bihar—was called *Madhyam Desh*. The name *Madhyadesh* likely originated from an adaptation of *Madhyam Desh*. The hilly regions of Garhwal and Kumaon, situated directly north of *Madhyadesh*, were not included in this designation. As a result, the people from these hilly areas referred to the southern plains as *Madhyadesh*, which eventually transformed into *Madhesh*.

Starting in the 15th century, Brahmins from Kumaon, including families like the Pandey and Panth, as well as local Kshatriyas such as Karki and Raut, migrated eastward and settled in regions ranging from Pyuthan to Dolakha. During this period, Ganesh Pandey, a commander under King Mukund Sen of Palpa, became a follower of King Drabya Shah of Gorkha. His Brahmin descendants continue to reside in Khoplang, Gorkha. Notable Kshatriya figures from this lineage, such as Kalu Pañdé and Damodar Pañdé, later gained prominence in Nepali history. These families, accustomed to calling the northern plains of North India *Madhesh*, applied the same term to the plains of Awadh and Bihar as they moved eastward, though this usage was somewhat misleading.

The flatlands bordering the Churé Hills to the north are

known as *Talahatti*, while the hilly and forested area between the Churé and Mahabharat ranges is called *Bhawar*. These two regions are commonly referred to together as *Terai*, a term that remains in use today.

However, Nepali officials have inaccurately classified both the flatlands of *Talahatti* and the hilly regions of *Bhawar* as part of *Madhesh*, resulting in an erroneous designation. This led to the creation of a separate office, *Madhesh Bandobast*, for land management, which was operational for many years but has since been dissolved. The Kumari Chowk office, established for accounting purposes, still includes a department called *Madhesh Faat* (Madhesh Zone). The term *Madhesh*, originally a shorthand for the region of *Madhyadesh* in the Gangetic and Yamunetic plains, is improperly used in the Kathmandu Valley. Therefore, it is crucial to eliminate the term 'Madhesh' from land management as soon as possible.

In ancient Nepal, the population was primarily concentrated between the Tamakoshi and Trishuli rivers, where the Newar ethnic group resided. The term *Nepar*, used to identify these original inhabitants, likely originated from the Magadhi pronunciation of *Nepali*, which locally evolved into *Newar*, carrying ethnic connotations. There is no historical evidence suggesting that the southern boundary of ancient Nepal extended beyond the Mahabharat range and its foothills.

King Manadeva (464–505 AD) of the Lichchhavi period, widely celebrated for his inscriptions at Changu, detailed his conquests and victories. However, these inscriptions do not suggest that his campaigns extended east of the Tamakoshi River. Instead, they mention crossing the Gandaki River to the west and securing victory in a place called *Mallapuri*, which brought significant wealth. It is my strong belief that *Mallapuri* could refer to a location in the Terai region across the Gandaki

River, possibly in the area around Butwal.

At the onset of the mediaeval period, after the valleys of Yenam and Kyirong opened, Nepal established diplomatic relations with Tibet and China. This expansion extended Nepal's influence into the northern Himalayan region, reaching nearly the current eastern boundary and extending westward to Sakhiko Lek. The famous Chinese traveller Xuanzang, who visited the region in 637 AD, provides evidence of this expansion. By the late mediaeval period, with the formation of the Sinja state west of Sakhiko Lek, the territory of present-day Butwal was incorporated into this state, as documented by the Rup Malla inscription of 1312 AD. Similarly, the Nanayadev inscription found in Simraungadh, Bara district, shows that the Terai region east of the Gandaki River was part of the Simraungadh state.

The fragmentation of the Nepalese state began in the 14th century due to internal conflicts among dynasties and foreign invasions. The fall of the Sinja state in Jumla led to the formation of separate states in Doti, marking a significant geographical decline for Nepal.

As Nepal began to disintegrate, the Khas people from the Sinja state migrated eastward and founded several small states. Consequently, the Nepalese state, originally centred around the Kathmandu Valley, eventually split into three distinct states: Kathmandu, Patan, and Bhaktapur. This fragmentation led to the exclusion of regions like Dolakha in the east and Gorkha in the west from the definition of Nepal. Thus, even at the dawn of the modern era, Nepal, like ancient times, remained confined to the region between the Sunkoshi and Trishuli rivers for nearly four centuries. During this period, the Newar settlements were primarily within this area, and the term 'Nepal' referred to the Newar ethnic group. By the late 18th century, the Newar language was still called the *Nepal Bhasa* (Nepal Language) in everyday usage. This term also extended internationally, where the *Nepal Sambat*, traditionally recognised as a Newar calendar, is often referred to as the *Newar Samvat* in contemporary writings.

From the latter half of the 11th century, Nepal played a crucial role in facilitating religious exchanges between Vikramashila in India and Buddhist monasteries in Tibet. During this time, the Buddhist monastery of Sa-Kya was established in 1076 AD on the eastern bank of the Brahmaputra, in a region known as *Chung*. This monastery developed close ties with the Nepali people. Due to the similarity in pronunciation between *Chung* and *Sang*, the Nepali people began referring to the inhabitants of that region as *Sang*. As a result, this term was also applied to people from other Tibetan regions. In the Newar language, Tibetans are still referred to as *Saṇ* or *Sã*.

King Prithvi Narayan Shah of the Gorkha state played a pivotal role in the unification of Nepal. Under his leadership, and that of his son, Crown Prince Bahadur Shah, Nepal was unified to include the hilly regions from the eastern Kirat region to the western Kumaon region, as well as the Himalayan regions and the Terai plains, forming the expansive Nepal Empire. Additionally, Sikkim and Garhwal were incorporated into the Nepalese realm. By 1804-1805 AD, the territory of the present-day Shimla extending from the Yamuna River to the Sutlej River was also included in the Nepalese state. The second edition of the *Encyclopedia Britannica*, published in 1811, illustrated the Nepalese Empire on its map, encompassing the area from the Teesta River in the east to the Sutlej River in the west, including the Himalayas, hills, and Terai.

Later, under the administration of Bhimsen Thapa, Nepal

lost significant territories, including the princely states of Sikkim, Kumaon, Garhwal, and Shimla, to the British following the war of 1815 AD. Additionally, the Terai region from Tal Baghaura to the Mahakali River was ceded, leaving the western part of Nepal fragmented. However, in 1860 AD, this fragmented area was reintegrated into Nepal under the name *Naya Muluk* (New Country), restoring the current boundaries of Nepal. Today, this territory is recognised as the Kingdom of Nepal both nationally and internationally.

Due to internal conflicts within the royal family, direct administration by the king lasted only about seven years (1836–1842 AD) between 1806 and 1950 AD. For the remaining 138 years, power was held by autocrats such as Bhimsen Thapa and Jung Bahadur, who ruled the Nepalese Empire through military force. Their primary objectives were to suppress national sentiments, misappropriate state funds, and reduce state revenue by redistributing land and resources among themselves, their families, and their loyalists. They centered their rule on the Kathmandu Valley, which covers approximately 250 square miles, calling it *Khaas Nepal* (Core Nepal), while treating the remaining 54,000 square miles of hills and Terai as colonial territories for exploitation. This policy led to the severe neglect of areas outside of *Khaas Nepal*.

Until 1815 AD, Gundri Bazar and Ilam Bazar were in similar conditions, but today, Gundri Bazar has evolved into the city of Darjeeling, while Ilam Bazar remains relatively undeveloped. A similar disparity exists between Almora and Siliguri. The Rana autocrats and their predecessors employed covert colonial strategies, creating a 'mini-Nepal' within Nepal itself—a country that was already internationally recognised. However, the true extent of this exploitation could not be entirely concealed.

We have already discussed the existence of a *Madhesh Faat* at the Kumari Chowk office earlier in this article. Similarly, a *Nepal Faat* (Nepal Zone) has also been established at these offices, specifically for managing records of offices within the Kathmandu Valley—a system that remains in place today. The Court Fee Act, intended for legal proceedings in Nepal, applies only to the Kathmandu Valley, thereby acknowledging only *Khaas Nepal* from a judicial perspective. Customs checks on goods carried by travellers entering or leaving the Kathmandu Valley are still enforced, and women require passports when travelling to or from other regions. In such a situation, how can people from outside the Kathmandu Valley identify themselves as Nepalese? European scholars have noted this colonial sentiment, and a recent map published in Roman script labels the Kathmandu Valley specifically as 'Nepal,' further distinguishing it as *Khaas Nepal*.

Forget far-flung areas—this colonial attitude even affects people from nearby places like Banepa, Dhulikhel, Chitlang, Nuwakot, and Sindhupalchok, who refer to their journey to the Kathmandu Valley as 'going to Nepal.' How can individuals from Darchula, Biratnagar, and Ilam feel pride in being Nepalese? Some, still caught in the charm of a colonial mindset and living in a bubble, insist that *Khaas Nepal* refers only to the Kathmandu Valley. May wisdom prevail! Only when Nepal witnesses good governance will true unification be achieved, thus ending colonialism and removing the stigma of being labelled an 'underdeveloped nation.' For now, that remains our hope. ◆

(This article is believed to have been written circa 1957 AD.)

MOUSTACHE

Hridaya Chandra Singh Pradhan

Just so folks don't think I'm making this up, I've got to admit: I've been obsessed with moustaches since my diaper days. I was totally mesmerised by the thick, black moustache my dad sported above his upper lip. Another reason I wanted a moustache? Pure jealousy. My dad adored me. Back then, I was his one and only lap warmer, and he showered me with all his affection. He'd kiss my cheeks whenever he got the chance, and I absolutely loved it. But his prickly moustache would poke me, making me a bit wary of his kisses.

Getting poked all the time by my dad's moustache made me want one of my own, so I could return the favour and poke him back with my kisses.

People are odd creatures; they hardly believe anything. I couldn't care less if they don't buy other people's stories. But if they doubt mine? Oh, that really gets my goat. Normally, my anger doesn't bother anyone, but sometimes I feel like going bonkers. I want to lose my mind and, in a whirlwind of madness, send those non-believers flying like leaves in a storm.

People argue against my claim, saying it's impossible to

think or remember things as a toddler, and even if you could, you wouldn't be able to recall them now. Damn such arguments. I firmly believe that a sharp memory makes anything possible. I once heard, and not just heard but learned from a reliable source, that Shree Nayab Badagurujyu Hemraj Pandit, also known as Shree Mahila Gurujyu, clearly remembered being fed by guests at his rice-feeding ceremony. Likewise, the famous Nepali poet and playwright, Shree Bal Krishna Jung Bahadur Rana, vividly remembered an incident from an age when he couldn't even speak, where his caretaker caused him discomfort. I heard this straight from the horse's mouth.

Ah, whatever! Believe it or not, the fact is, ever since I started crawling and cradling, I wanted a moustache above my lip. By the time I was 8 or 9 years old, my desire for a moustache had only grown stronger. One reason was that a thick, bristly moustache supposedly made a man's wife fear and obey him more—at least, that's what I heard from many people. Another perk of a moustache, they said, was that everyone fears a moustachioed man.

From a young age, I had a burning desire to rule over my wife and intimidate everyone with a grand moustache. I believed that to truly enjoy life, you had to be high and mighty. I thought having a moustache, that ultimate symbol of power, would let me indulge in pleasures without lifting a finger. Ever since childhood, I wanted to enjoy life's fruits while making others carry the burden, whether that workhorse was my wife or someone else. I saw the moustache as a crucial natural weapon for achieving this. And I figured that's why women didn't have moustaches and men did—men had the birthright to wield absolute authority over women and command their service. The moustache was the badge of this authority. This belief made me desperate to grow up and sprout a moustache as quickly as possible, thinking it would earn me serious respect.

Every day, I'd check the mirror, eagerly searching for the first signs of a moustache. After years of waiting, when I turned 18, a faint moustache line finally appeared. For days, I jumped around with excitement, not caring about much else. I started applying all sorts of coloured oils and remedies to boost its growth and thickness. My days were spent discussing with others and hunting for ways to speed up the process.

As my efforts paid off, my moustache grew thicker, and so did my confidence and pride. With every new inch of whisker, I felt my authority and vanity grow, and I started commanding respect and admiration everywhere I went. Since my moustache appeared, my sense of superiority swelled. My right hand was constantly busy stroking it, and I felt like the world was at my feet. In those moments, I often imagined myself as the greatest of all.

My moustache scared the daylights out of people. Even my acquaintances would tremble with fear when I stroked my moustache and shot them a stern look. For some reason, stroking the moustache seemed to add a touch of grandeur and anger to my disposition. So, whether I was moving, sitting, or lying down, you could always catch me tugging at my moustache. My wife, siblings, and even my most trusted associates were so intimidated that they hesitated to speak up about things that might earn them praise, fearing my reaction.

While people feared me because of my moustache, they didn't miss a chance to laugh at it behind my back. One day, noticing my unusually happy mood, my wife cautiously remarked, "Your moustache doesn't really suit you. It's grown so long! Maybe you could shave it off. It's the latest trend, after all."

Since I was in high spirits, I couldn't help but chuckle at her comment. She looked astonished, probably expecting me to stroke my moustache and get mad. Instead, I laughed and said, "Does a real man ever shave his moustache? We're lucky to have them. Do you think you could ever grow a moustache, even if you wanted to? A man without a moustache is considered unmanly."

Although I could silence my wife with macho talk about moustaches, her comment initially rattled me. I started scrutinising myself in the mirror and realised that my moustache did look out of place. On my short and lean body, the long, thick moustache seemed rather ridiculous. I worried it was longer than my body! Plus, it was a multi-coloured mess, with patches of black, grey, dark brown, light brown, and various other shades, making it look disjointed and unkempt. I feared that if I kept it, I might end up looking like a circus act to children.

From that point on, my moustache and I were at odds. I had a major dilemma. As a devoted son, I remembered the saying, "One who has their parents alive should never shave their moustache," and I held onto this belief like it was the gospel truth. This internal tug-of-war between my desires and my beliefs started to drive me nuts. I disliked my moustache so much that I wanted to pluck every hair and toss them all away. I became obsessed, diving into classical texts, and considering scientific and psychological takes on moustaches. Despite all my research, I couldn't find a good reason to keep it. I started seeing my belief in the moustache as a symbol of filial piety as nothing more than superstition.

One day, with the utmost humility, I approached my parents and asked, "My moustache has become a wild, varicoloured mess. Nowadays, everyone trims their moustaches. Can I trim mine too?" My father, with loving concern, replied, "I care about your heart, not your face. If your heart holds devotion, the appearance of your moustache doesn't matter. A long moustache might scream 'Look at me, I'm pious!' but it doesn't show true devotion. Kids could still be treating their parents badly behind the scenes. So, I want to reside in your heart, not in your moustache."

I also found immense truth in my father's words. I was astonished that even someone from ancient times like him would resonate with such modern ideas. I was half-expecting him to suggest I should tackle my inner demons with a razor. What more could I ask for? I got the green light. Thrilled, I had the whole beard shaved off on the spot.

After ditching the moustache, I felt like a whole new person. My face seemed to morph from a ghastly horror show to something divine—calm and serene. I began to admire my reflection obsessively. My habit of gazing into the mirror grew day by day. I was amazed that, without the moustache, my face appeared more serene and thoughtful, and my heart seemed to embrace humility and peace. People who used to tremble in my presence were now chatting openly and giving advice. Shaving off my moustache brought about a profound, peaceful transformation. As my demeanour shifted towards tranquillity, the world and life seemed to bloom in beauty.

I started shaving every day. Just like defecating and bathing, I began to see shaving as an essential part of my hygiene routine. I made it my first task of the morning, believing it would help me cultivate tranquillity. By making shaving my priority, I found that it set a peaceful tone for my day. Seeing my face first thing in the morning allowed me to check in with an expression of joy, decorum, serenity, and humility. If I saw anything less, I felt a bit embarrassed and regretful, but it pushed me towards a more virtuous and beautiful outlook. Shaving made me look in the mirror more often, something I didn't do much with the moustache, and I found great pleasure in this ritual. I realised that our faces mirror our inner emotions—our efforts to lean towards the 'good' and away from the 'bad' are reflected there.

The idea that "stroking a moustache enhances vigour and thought" isn't quite accurate. It's like how smokers praise tobacco—just a habit, really. I find that closing my eyes can also make me feel more energetic and thoughtful. But if someone tried to mimic my habit by walking around with their eyes closed, they'd just end up bumping into things.

Some people argue that shaving a moustache is a sign of becoming feminine or emasculated, or that it makes you a wimp or henpecked. It's baffling why women are looked down upon this way since I've seen plenty of grace and beauty in them. The qualities of decorum, dignity, humility, gentleness, and non-violence—so often missing in men—shine brightly in women.

We all seek happiness, peace, and joy—these are the true essence of life and humanity. If our environment were peaceful, we wouldn't need swords, guns, cannons, or bombs. Yet, we continue to rely on these violent tools for peacekeeping, while ignoring our own role in the problem. With virtue, beauty, sweet speech, and polite behaviour, we could find heaven in every step. Every moment of life could bring joy to our friends and acquaintances. These qualities are often more pronounced in women than in men. If we truly value virtues over mere labels, we should look to the virtues found in women, as well as in the animals and birds around us.

Indeed, a moustache often symbolises dominance, vanity, and vigour. This might explain why women, who generally lack moustaches, are sometimes perceived as less assertive or dominant. In the animal kingdom, males with long whiskers are often seen as the most dominant and formidable. Similarly, men's nature seems more peaceful and attractive before the moustache appears; once it does, it often brings a touch of unruliness. There's even a legend that women with moustaches are harsh. Among deities, those with moustaches, like Shiva, are depicted as fierce and wrathful, whereas deities like Vishnu, Narayana, Ram, Krishna, and Buddha, known for their peaceful nature, are clean-shaven. This might be why they are associated with the preservation and beauty of creation.

In reality, a face without a moustache looks more delicate, gentle, and humble. The desire to avoid struggle often leads people to seek peace. Although the struggle has been part of human tradition for ages, people are increasingly looking for ways to preserve their peace. Noting the decreased struggle and increased virtue among women, it seems that men are now trying to emulate these qualities by shaving their moustaches. Since we're not inclined towards the more destructive scientific attitudes seen in some cultures, we might achieve greater virtue by embracing the positive qualities associated with women, starting with shaving our moustaches. In my view, civilisation might have subtly guided humanity towards this tradition of shaving as a measure of civility.

Masculinity doesn't have to mean dominating or bringing others down through sheer force. If that's what masculinity entails, then I'd rather pass on it. If a moustache is seen as a symbol of such traits, then being a man seems like a raw deal. If masculinity is about self-esteem, pride, and dignity, then femininity, which embodies these qualities too, deserves equal respect.

If shaving off a moustache leads to being seen as

henpecked, that's not a bad thing at all. It's better to be a morally upright, happy "henpecked" man than to constantly mistreat your wife. If a wife is devoted to her husband, there's nothing wrong with the husband being devoted—or even a bit henpecked. In fact, it's a sign of refinement.

I once heard a tale, though I can't vouch for its accuracy. It claims that in ancient times, men who engaged in theft, robbery, and mischief were clean-shaven, leading men to start honouring moustaches.

Honestly, I find moustaches repulsive. The breath that comes from a bearded mouth and the dust and dirt that cling to it are just gross to me.

Some argue that a moustache acts as a gatekeeper for the nose, keeping dust out. Such beliefs might imply that God is unjust or biased since women don't have moustaches. Does this mean their noses don't need gatekeepers and they should somehow fend off dust on their own to stay healthy? Men aren't born with moustaches; it takes at least fifteen years for one to grow long enough to act as a proper gatekeeper. Until then, men should have been constantly ill from dust.

To me, a moustache is simply a sign of aging. As we grow older, our moustaches get longer and more twisted, signalling the coming of old age, and ultimately death. Therefore, removing this symbol of aging seems like a way to embrace youth and extend longevity. ◆

ABSTRACT THOUGHT: AN ONION

Shankar Lamichhane

Last evening, I ran into Bangdelji[1] at New Road. He said, "Shankarji, I read your article, 'Shankar Lamichhane in the eyes of Shankar Lamichhane.'"

"What did you think?" I asked.

"Very nice. It's quite realistic. Now, try something abstract."

"That's your job! Why should I switch to painting now?"

"No, no, not that—I mean use an abstract style in your writing."

I just kept smiling. (Knowing how to smile is quite an art! As a person ages, their smile gains new shades of meaning.) Smiling, I bid Bangdelji goodbye and subtly changed the topic.

In Vyathitji's[2] hands was the cover of the literary magazine Himani. At a glance, one could recognise Bangdel's brushwork, just as the name Himani instantly brought Vyathit's writing to mind. He would often say, "Someone like you, whose pen flows

---

[1] Lain Singh Bangdel was a renowned Nepali artist, writer, and art historian, celebrated for his contributions to modern Nepali art.

[2] Kedar Man Vyathit was a prominent Nepali poet, writer, and political activist known for his contributions to Nepali literature. He was the editor of Himani.

so well, please write a story for Himani in a day or two. I'm going abroad to get it printed and aim to release it on Vijaya Dashami."

I just kept smiling. (Knowing how to smile is quite an art! Not knowing how to smile at the right time can be as worse as crying.) Smiling, I bid Vyathitji goodbye and subtly changed the topic.

But neither Vyathit nor Bangdel left my thoughts; neither did Himani nor the abstract! The mind is a curious thing. Once something enters it, it's hard to get rid of. If you try, it's like a clash between your personality and the thing itself. What enters the mind never comes out the same way—it transforms. So, I began to sift through my thoughts, wondering just how much stuff was moving around in there.

Vyathitji! Just as Lord Krishna showed his mother Yasodha his universal form *(Vishwaroop)* by opening his mouth wide, today I invite you to see my universal form. Glance into my universe and understand what's on my mind. But first, let me remind you of a few things. I am a twentieth-century thinker, a middle-class man, married with children, young and healthy, deeply involved in creative thoughts, and an ordinary citizen of my country. And yes, I have many problems.

My biggest problem is that I'm standing on no man's land. On one side is the faith of my forefathers, and on the other, the beliefs of my offspring. I feel elated at the launch of Sputnik and derive immense pride when I hear they've planted the hammer-and-sickle printed Russian flag on the moon's dust, as if Khrushchev had borrowed it from my own home. Yet, when there's a lunar eclipse, I worry about pregnant women touching me and atone by distributing alms to the sweeper's caste, as though King Manu himself were the patriarch of my Lamichhane clan.

For the sake of staying informed, I read all sorts of papers—from Gorkhapatra to the Times, News Weekly to Filmfare, and even Rómance. I try to absorb every bit of news, and I've been doing this for a while. My mind is crowded with events like Marilyn Monroe's suicide and Elizabeth Taylor's latest love troubles. There's the death of Dag Hammarskjöld, the workings of the UN, U Thant, the Cold War between the USSR and USA, and issues in Laos, Suez, Galwan Valley, Kashmir, Malaya, Eritrea, and Ceylon. All these problems swirl around in my head.

I read Henry Miller's *Tropic of Cancer* and wonder where I can find Capricorn now. Sir Winston Churchill's thigh bone is broken—will it heal? What will Nepal present to the UN this time? How will Congo fare in the voting? My son, who was suffering from typhoid, has recovered, but I'm not sure if meat is available in the market today. They say today and tomorrow are *Ekadashi*—an auspicious day when Hindus are supposed to avoid meat.

A scientist has succeeded in extracting milk from grass, anti-national elements have crossed the border and opened fire, there was an attempted assassination on the President of France, and how will the Algerian problem be resolved? Albert Camus, also an Algerian, is someone I'm currently reading—*The Myth of Sisyphus*. A Telstar satellite has made television broadcasting in Europe possible. A peasant across the farm, who used to ask me in Newari[3], *"Ja-nae-dun-la bajya"* (Have you had your meal, sir?), has passed away. He had no children. Bangdel, who also has no children, asks me to write abstractly, just like the cover art of Himani, in the style of Vyathit's language...

---

[3] Newari refers to the language and cultural traditions of the Newar, an indigenous ethnic group of the Kathmandu Valley, known for their rich art, culture, and architecture.

I find myself in no man's land, right in the middle of such conflicting thoughts. See, Vyathits and Bangdels, my life itself is an abstract mess. I keep pushing it away every day. My mornings start with thoughts of needing money for groceries, my afternoons are spent searching for ways to make money, and my evenings end with exhaustion. Every day, my acquaintances die here and there, and I spend time forgetting their passing. I remember a part of the history, sketch out the future, and evaluate a piece of the present—all on a daily basis.

Every day involves haggling, buying, selling, and dealing with the mortgage and interest on my faith, beliefs, desires, and ambitions. "Sukucha, the butcher, must have tricked our servant; today's meat is just bones. The milk is so watery today. The firewood is both damp and overpriced!"—these are the endless complaints from the housewife, the children, and the cook that fill my mind.

On top of that, I add my own worries: Nehru spoke in Parliament today—how much of it was true? What will Khrushchev's new moves against Berlin mean for the world? If a world war breaks out, where will it start? How many children's lives will be ruined by the effects of Thalidomide? And where has Alfred Noyes ended up? They say he wanted to die in the mountains!

Bangdelji, whose life isn't abstract? Whose life isn't despicable—unless he hides his stench in silence? Whose feelings aren't contemptible—unless he buries them under a facade of smiles? Whose heart isn't full of greed—unless it's subdued by slogans? Vyathitji, the age of the ancient sages is long gone. Now, every conscious mind is as complex as Lord Krishna's cosmic form.

Today's person is like a God—one who creates his own world through schemes, deception, treachery, murder, laws, irresponsibility, superstition, worship, honour, and folly. And today's God isn't bound by any religion. He finds rivals in Christ, Mohammad, and Buddha. Today's God is as diplomatic as priests—something like: "O Holy Priest! Why don't we do it this way?" "Sure, sure, why not?"

Today's God is also an atheist like Buddha. And today's god is controlled by people—much like birth control pills. You want a god, and he's right there; you don't, and he vanishes! He can appear in any quantity you need. For poetry, He's in metrical form. For eulogies, He's a lexicon. For toadies, He's an encyclopaedia. In Urdu, He's 'garibparbar'; in Sanskrit, 'karunanidhan'; in pure Bhanubhakta[4] Nepali, 'khwamit'...

Yes, today's man has become a God himself, possessing all the qualities of a deity—except one. He has lost the quality of being truly human—a real person who remains human until death and dies as a man.

Vyathitji and Bangdelji, if you're looking for someone who's lost their humanity but hasn't quite reached godhood, come to me. You won't find anyone more inhuman than me, and unlike me, others won't openly admit it. What can I do, Vyathitji? I'm not calling myself inhuman out of anger. Look, I'm a Hindu and naturally I love all Hindu gods, but I also have fondness for Christ, Buddha, and Mohammad.

I appreciate all faiths in the name of God and all the atrocities committed in their names. Without those crusades, the attacks on Shankaracharya, Ashoka's missionary victories, and Tuglag Shah's jihads[5], how could Vyathits today be Hindus, Bangdels Christians, and Shankars Muslims? I might have ended up as someone who believes in everything but honours nothing. So how could I chant 'Aham Brahmasmi' (I am divine

---

[4] Bhanubhakta Acharya, known as Aadi Kavi (The First Poet), was a pioneering Nepali poet who translated the Ramayana from Sanskrit into Nepali.
[5] Jihad is an Islamic term for spiritual or moral struggle, sometimes interpreted as a fight for a religious cause.

consciousness) if I believed in everyone else but not in myself?

I'm not the man of today, Vyathitji! I'm a person who'll be born a thousand years from now. In my time, there will be no borders between nations, no boundaries of faith, religion, or politics—nothing at all.

Let me explain why I stand on this no man's land today. I don't want to fit into your categories or colours. If I cross the border, I'd have to choose a citizenship—so I prefer to remain a non-citizen. I am a border myself, separating the present from the past and the past from the future.

You must have seen borders. In the middle of no man's land stands a mysterious five-mouthed *linga*[6] that no one offers holy bael leaves to. Yet, moving or removing it would require the sacrifice of many lives. What colour is this border, Bangdelji? White, like Shiva's tresses? Grey, like the soil? Red, like in maps? Fluid, like rivers? Invisible, like mountain peaks? Oh, Bangdelji! If you are able to paint these borderlines abstractly, then I will certainly paint my mind in abstract thoughts too.

Until you capture that and complete it, I'll remain unexpressed. If I present myself abstractly today, you'd need to breathe in the Parisian air again to understand it. To decipher my abstract portrayal, you'll need to memorise the line "Probably one day" once more.

That's why I smile.

And because of this, my smile has many layers—one for Vyathit, one for Bangdel, another for my son, and so on.

I continue to live because I've portrayed others and myself realistically.

In reality, I'm like an onion—colourless, layered, with a boundless stench and deep complexity.

---

[6] In Hindu culture, the linga is a symbolic representation of Lord Shiva, often depicted as a cylindrical stone or pillar, signifying his divine energy and presence.

The cosmic form of Krishna today is like an onion. So, Bangdelji, please create a still-life portrait of an onion. Vyathitji, kindly write an epic about onions. Such a creation will be historic because the stench of today's man and society will be preserved in its endless layers forever. I will also live on in that portrait and epic for eternity.

If this portrait and poetry aren't created now, future generations will lose today's history once Himani, Bangdel, and Shankar are gone.

...just as all borders will disappear a thousand years from now. ◆

FROM BRAHMA'S LABORATORY

Bhairav Aryal

"Argh!" Brahmaji[1] grumbled as he lazily perched on top of the newly formed Himalayas. "Some places are so high they almost touch the sky, and others are so low they reach the depths. I've put so much effort into creating this Earth, yet it's still so lumpy and uneven."

No matter how hard he tried, he couldn't smooth out the Earth's bumpy surface, which left old Brahmaji feeling exasperated. He thought to himself, "The sky is perfectly even, the underworld is perfectly even, but the Earth I made looks like a crumpled piece of paper!"

"What kind of creature can I possibly create on such a bumpy Earth?" Brahmaji wondered. "Won't my own creations mock me and ask, 'Why would someone who can't even make a smooth surface try to create life?'"

Feeling a pang of guilt, Brahmaji sighed deeply. "Never mind the unevenness," he thought, "but the Earth had to be strong and unfaltering. Yet, with just a gust of wind, it shakes from top to bottom. A stronger earthquake could crumble it to

---

[1] In Hindu mythology, Brahma is the creator god, responsible for the creation of the universe and all living beings.

pieces. It's always at risk of cracking open. If the Earth itself is so unstable, what hope is there for those who live on it? If the Earth is so fragile, how can anything survive here?"

Like a mason disheartened by the tottering house he built, or a painter distraught by his deformed painting, or a scientist disappointed by a flawed invention, Brahmaji looked at his creation, Earth, and declared, "To hell with it!"

But after a while, the fresh mountain breeze on the snowy peak calmed Brahmaji's troubled mind. Feeling a bit better, he thought, "Alright, let this Earth stay uneven. Let the peaks be shaky. I'll create a creature with knowledge, wisdom, and strength. I'll call this creation 'Man.' And this Man will make the uneven Earth smooth. He'll strengthen the foundation and adorn it with the prosperity of heaven, fulfilling my creative pursuit. Yes, I'll create Man, blending my utmost strength and skills. He will be my heir, superior to myself!"

Stroking his white beard, Brahmaji smiled and rising from his spot, he ambled down the foothills. Wandering around the Himalayas, Brahmaji gathered various materials: loads of gold, cement, and cotton fluff. His task was to create a man who could smooth out the uneven Earth, sustain creation forever, and lead the way.

As he worked with the gold, a doubt surfaced: "What if I can't bring this man to life? What then? Maybe I should run a small test first." So, he mixed a handful of earth with water to create a mortar. From this mix, he fashioned a pair of legs, wings, a pointed beak, and a body. He wrapped the creation in cotton fluff and painted it with molten gold and copper. The result was a bizarre sight. Brahmaji couldn't help but laugh at it.

But this wasn't surprising. Like a potter testing his wheel with a misshapen pot before crafting something beautiful, Brahmaji was merely experimenting. So, he blew life into his odd creation from both ends of its beak and bottom. As he did, the creature flapped its wings and crowed, "Cock-a-doodle-doo."

Brahmaji smiled, reassured that he could infuse life into his creations.

***

Today, Brahmaji's laboratory in the high Himalayan cavern was a scene of chaos. On one side, there were meticulously crafted body parts—hands, legs, heads, backbones, ribs—all made from the toughest materials, designed to fit together perfectly, and piled up in an artistic mess. On the other side, gold was being melted. Brahmaji, overwhelmed, was juggling his attention between these tasks, all while cutting the most brilliant gems to design the eyes.

Everything was set. Brahmaji began assembling the parts. He attached heads on all four sides, just like his own, and decided to add four legs and four hands, thinking this creature would need extra limbs to tackle the uneven Earth.

He carefully put together a body with a golden mortar, pearl eyes, a mercury brain, and a cotton fluff heart, all encased in a solid metal shell. Then he added wings, thinking the creature should be able to fly to the heavens. In no time, his creation was complete, looking just as he envisioned.

Brimming with joy, Brahmaji examined each organ and found everything perfectly in place. It seemed poised to flap its wings, walk on its legs, and talk right away. What a work of art! Brahmaji couldn't help but pat himself on the back.

After a while, Brahmaji placed the man at the cave's entrance and filled every part with life. The man was finally complete, and Brahma's dream seemed fulfilled. Eager to see his creation come to life, Brahmaji called out affectionately, "My dear man! Oh dear man!"

But the man remained silent. Brahmaji raised his voice and tried again, "Hey man!" Still, no response. Frustration set in as Brahmaji's forehead began to sweat and his limbs grew numb. He had created such a beautiful, strong man, yet it didn't utter a single word. "Good grief!" he exclaimed.

Brahmaji's determination wasn't about to wane after just one failure. The next day, he had a new creation in the lab. This time, it had three mouths instead of four heads and was made with a lighter build. He placed it out in the yard and called out, "Oh dear man! Oh darling man!"

But again, there was no response from any of the three mouths. Brahmaji was deeply discouraged by this second failure. In a fit of rage, he even considered setting the lab on fire and going off to meditate.

Sitting dejectedly on the ground, he sighed and thought, "Let's try a different approach. This time, I'll use a steel frame with copper mortar." He decided to forgo the wings and give the new creation just two mouths—one at the front and one at the back. The next day, the copper man stood ready before Brahmaji. Once more, Brahmaji blew life into the creation and called, "Oh dear man! Oh darling man!" But once again, the man remained silent.

As the saying goes, "In for a penny, in for a pound," Brahmaji thought, "Let's try something new with this hen's droppings." He gathered the droppings in frustration, mixed them with ashes from the furnace, and applied this concoction to a rough wooden frame. The result was a structure with droopy hands and feet, a lopsided face, hair all over, a tangle of tresses on the head, and a comically large nose between the mouth and eyes. The whole thing looked absurd.

"Ugh! What a horrible figure! Can a man ever look like this? It seems like if life were pumped into it from the front, it would just leak out from the back. If the better ones didn't speak, how could this monstrosity possibly talk?" Brahmaji was filled with disgust and disdain for his fourth experiment.

"Just like the uneven Earth, so is the uneven man! Perfect match, old Brahma. Maybe you should shave off your beard and give it to this guy too," Brahmaji joked, poking fun at himself. "If this monstrosity somehow speaks, I'll make another one to be its partner and split the reproductive powers between them. That would be quite a sight. This poor creature, even as a whole, would always be half. Then I wouldn't have to keep creating new men over and over."

With that thought, Brahmaji reluctantly gave life to the grotesque structure. He didn't hold out any hope that this creation would speak, but he figured there was no harm in finishing the ritual. Settling down on a mound, he called out in a dismissive tone, like a wealthy person addressing a servant, "Hey man, you worthless piece of junk!"

Before Brahmaji's voice even faded, the bizarre creation responded with a hung head, "Yes, sir!"

This enraged Brahmaji, who felt the voice was mocking him. In a fit of fury, he snapped, "May you die, you fool!"

And what a mess that created! Here was a creature made from chicken droppings and ashes, and Brahmaji had just cursed it to death. How could such a ridiculous being ever help realise Brahmaji's dream of making the Earth even?

Like an old madman, Brahmaji burst into laughter and vanished. His absurd experiment, 'Man', was born and died repeatedly on this uneven Earth, continuing the cycle till date.

Don't believe it? Just scratch your skin, and you'll find dirt that's a mix of chicken droppings and ashes. ◆

DEITIES IN RIGVEDA

Pradeep Nepal

I do not claim to be a Sanskrit scholar, so I cannot state with conviction that what follows is the absolute truth. I hold Sanskrit literature in high regard and deeply regret not having studied it in the past. In Nepal, the study of Sanskrit has often been undervalued. However, observing the respect for Sanskrit education in France and Germany brings to mind the adage, "He who lives near the shrine is often far from God."

The origins of the Sanskrit language are rooted in the Vedas, which are often referred to as the repository of knowledge. These texts are not the work of a single author but rather a compendium of songs spanning from the earliest days of civilisation to the period when they spread beyond the Sindhu River. It is more accurate to view the Vedas as a collection of folk songs reflecting various epochs and peoples, rather than merely as Sanskrit hymns and mantras.

Our ancestors rendered the Vedas almost sacrosanct, transforming them into mantras and using them as instruments for making a living. As a result, in regions like Nepal and India, the Vedas have been neglected, while universities in Germany and France have pursued serious studies of Sanskrit. This disparity in intellectual advancement between Europeans and South Asians can be partly attributed to the marginalisation and neglect of Sanskrit education in South Asia.

There is a common misconception that the Vedas are synonymous with Hinduism. In truth, the Vedas represent knowledge and education while Hinduism is a vast and evolving cultural phenomenon, absorbed and reinterpreted through various cultural lenses over time. Hinduism does not conform to the rigid structures of other religions and lacks the religious fanaticism often associated with them. A Hindu might abstain from eating pork or consume it, uphold the caste system or oppose it, revere cows or eat them, and choose to wear or forgo the *tika*. This flexibility and diversity make Hinduism a uniquely pluralistic tradition.

In our present discussion, the focus is not on Hinduism as a whole but rather on the concept of deities.

In Hindu tradition, Brahma is revered as the meta-father, the great creator, and a principal deity. However, the Vedas depict Brahma differently. For example, one Vedic passage describes Brahma as follows: "O Indra, those who honour you hold you in high esteem and offer you respect through the recitation of mantras. Just as an acrobat or dancer performs feats on bamboo poles, the priest called Brahma exalts you with grand hymns of praise."

Tilak Prasad Luintel's Nepali translation of the *Rigveda* quotes a reference on page 8 that does not regard Brahma as a deity. However, presenting only this excerpt may lead to confusion, potentially portraying Indra as the primary deity. Therefore, a brief exploration of Indra's role is also warranted for clarity.

The Vedas reference Indra extensively, depicting him in various roles: as Shatakratu, the performer of a hundred sacrifices; as the chief of cowherds; as the leader of farmers; and as *Gananayak*, the leader of groups. A scholarly examination of these references suggests that Indra, long regarded as the king of gods, symbolises a class of prominent individuals who played a crucial role in civilisation following the decline of matriarchy. Just as ancient rulers in Nepal were termed kings, the leaders or chiefs of antiquity were known as Indra.

This portrayal is underscored by hymns celebrating his deeds, such as: "O Indra, wielder of the thunderbolt, extend our wealth in all directions like cows released from the pen," "O Indra, you vanquished the demon who stole the cows; the gods, having been defeated by the demons, turned to you for assistance," "O Indra, in battle, your renown spreads from the earth to the heavens (implying the universe)," "O Indra, may our praises from all directions enhance your lifespan and glory." "O priests, offer this *Soma* (alcohol) to invigorate the strength of Indra who holds the ability to fulfil all tasks."

The *Rigveda* thus contains numerous references depicting Indra as a formidable human figure, endowed with strength and intelligence but devoid of supernatural or miraculous attributes. This suggests that Indra symbolises the patriarchal lineage established after the decline of matriarchy, as represented in the Vedic tradition.

Nevertheless, the *Rigveda* does include references to deities. For instance, on page 11, Usha, the dawn, is invited to the *yajna* (sacred sacrifice) as a goddess. On page 21, Varuna, the deity of water, is honoured with the invocation: "O Lord Varuna, we praise you with mantras." Agni, the god of fire, receives frequent praise, as noted on page 22: "Among the immortal gods, let us first praise Lord Agni." The Earth is also revered as a goddess on page 18: "O Mother Earth, you are the source of joy. You have the power to remove obstacles and provide a splendid abode."

In essence, the Rigveda places high reverence on Usha, Earth, the Sun, Agni, and Varuna among its deities. These elements were vital to ancient life: Usha brought light, Earth provided a place to live, the Sun offered warmth, Agni enhanced the flavour of food, and water was essential for sustaining life. As reflected on page 20, "Water has qualities like nectar and medicinal properties. Gods, be fervent in praising such water," our ancestors revered these natural elements as deities, given their limited understanding of the natural world.

Up until roughly fifty years ago, the practice of venerating physical objects as deities was prevalent. For instance, in Nepal, women traditionally worshipped the moon as a deity on every full moon day. Even now, some rural communities believe that water becomes impure during an eclipse.

Hinduism is often said to encompass 330 million gods and goddesses—a reflection of the peculiar and superstitious aspects of South Asian feudalism. As Sanskrit became increasingly inaccessible, new deities emerged in localities, and priests wove this proliferation into a complex web of superstition. Our ancestors erred by portraying the Vedas, with their rich heritage, as esoteric knowledge reserved for the elite and inaccessible to Shudras and women. Instead of being viewed as a repository of knowledge, the Vedas were misrepresented as portals to heaven and hell. Rather than applying scientific analysis to ancient wisdom, past leaders enshrouded it in mystery.

The feudal agenda to portray kings as incarnations of Vishnu was notably successful. The rule that kings should be primary patrons of *shakti peethas* (sacred shrines in Shaktism) effectively transformed them into deities. To reinforce this notion, there was a deliberate attempt to obscure the material aspects of Vedic hymns, making them appear immaterial and further entrenching the divine status of kings in the public consciousness.

This misguided approach has distanced us from our own history, leading to the unwarranted suppression of Eastern philosophy. True knowledge was obscured while falsehoods were elevated. It is imperative for our generation to correct this course.

On a lighter note, here's a humorous anecdote: During the *bratabandha* (sacred thread ceremony), the priest would recite Gayatri Mantra. There was a belief that if someone who hadn't undergone the ceremony heard the mantra, both the listener and the reciter would go mad. As I hadn't undergone the ceremony, my friends would playfully approach me, pretending to chant in an incomprehensible language, and mock me. Fifteen years later, I discovered that the same mantra—*oṃ bhūr bhuvaḥ svaḥ tat savitur vareṇyaṃ bhargo devasya dhīmahi dhiyo yo naḥ prachodayāt* (Let us meditate on the magnificent glory of the divine Sun, may He enlighten our minds)—was posted on the streets of Banaras. Today, this once-forbidden mantra is set to music and broadcast on radios across Nepal as a tribute to the Earth.

Knowledge is indeed vast and profound, yet it is within our grasp. Eastern philosophy has the potential to elevate society from ignorance and superstition to wisdom and material understanding. ◆

I'LL COME WITH FLOWERS

Sudha Tripathi

Sunkhani, my birthplace, you may feel I have forsaken my love for you. It's obvious, given that even now, as I near the twilight of my youth, I have not yet done anything significant for you. I hear that you often raise your hand to your forehead, standing on tiptoe, and squint towards the hills of Dolakha, searching for me.

I have not abandoned my love for you, Sunkhani. To forsake my love for you would be to forsake myself, for you are the essence of who I am. My dear Sunkhani! Deep within my heart, I am drenched in your kindness and affection. Tell me, how else could I survive in this barren desert if not for you?

I will never ask you not to wait for me, though it seems I still have some distance to cover before I can return to play in your lap. What can a humble daughter offer to your reverence? What do I have? Yet, I am rich in emotion. I wish to offer a handful of white blooms at your sacred feet. Although I have searched through the vastness of this city, I have yet to gather a a single handful of those white flowers that bloom in the pure lands of the heart.

My desire has always been to see you adorned with flowers at least once in this lifetime! But it seems the roots of these pure white blooms are being devoured by poisonous pests. Tell me, Sunkhani, when will my hands be filled? When will I feel your touch and affection once more?

There are moments when I want to distance myself from you, to lose myself in the sanctuary of your memory, never to meet or see you again. For there is a certain sweetness in pain and an irresistible allure in dreams. Sometimes, it feels more comforting to love from afar than to risk resentment up close. From a distance, everything appears more beautiful; the closer you get, the more imperfections reveal themselves. Watching roses from afar might make you want to live and die around them. Even if you must leave the barren city, your heart still yearns to be near those roses, to touch them. Yet, those who are captivated by beauty often become reckless and wild. They cling to the roses, only to be pricked by the thorns and appalled by the harsh reality. Beauty, it seems, can be a deceptive trap.

Therefore, Sunkhani, I see people through the lens of flowers. I see their lives marked by pain. I see my village and my country in fragments, and within those fragments, I find reflections of your life and suffering. You are the mirror through which I see my country. You are the faith of my existence. You are my small nation, my little world.

Yet, Sunkhani, I worship you with heartfelt devotion. But lately, an inexplicable fear grips me at the thought of drawing near to you. I fear that your imperfections may shatter the fragile edge of my faith, sending me tumbling down the precipice of belief. My journey towards you may remain unfinished, weighed down by the burden of doubt that cripples my steps.

How can I distance myself from you without ever drawing near? I laugh with the fragrance of your soil in my hands, living with your breath coursing through my being. Your Tamakoshi river flows through my veins. I need not say much; just catching a glimpse of Gaurishankar from this desert makes my hands instinctively reach out to you. Yes, Sunkhani! Seeing Gaurishankar stirs a deep emotion within me, bringing tears to my eyes, as if I am melting like wax touched by fire. Gaurishankar evokes countless warm memories we shared, as though the babbling words of my childhood echo from its towering peaks. The sight of its snow-white bosom recalls the butter lumps you fed me in your lap. The glacial lines of Gaurishankar bring back the taste of curd, dripping through the spaces between my fingers as I held it in my hands.

I wish to place you at the threshold of my past, even if just for a moment. When I recall that memory, tears and smiles blend on my face. I was young then—one day, for reasons I can no longer remember, you raised your hand in anger. But before it could strike my cheek, it softened into a gentle caress. I remember bursting into tears and, in my childish rage, I struck you back with my tiny fists. You can't be easily forgotten, my land, my Sunkhani! My precious treasure of love!

Every time I taste the tangy, bittersweet orange slices from foreign lands, I am reminded of the juicy, sweet oranges you once fed me. My mouth waters at the thought. Even as I eat these imported oranges, it's your oranges that fill my memories with their true sweetness. The water in Kathmandu tastes so different—it's simply incomparable. I think even the buffaloes of Sunkhani would refuse it. I close my eyes, trying to summon the taste of the pristine water of Tamakoshi as I reluctantly sip this city water.

This life, your precious gift, erodes as it grates against the stony heart of Kathmandu. I live in constant fear that I may never return this gift to you. If only I could offer it back to you before this body collapses, my deepest longing would be fulfilled. How could Kathmandu, this barren city, ever return it whole? It will surely grind away the beauty you bestowed upon me. But I will return, Mother, without fail. Do not despair. Do not shed tears when you see my bedraggled state. Do not let your eyes well up at the sight of my erratic heartbeat—the heart you so lovingly nurtured.

Physical beauty is not life's entirety; a person's heart must never grow ugly. This city's harshness may have marred this body, but my heart remains as you made it. Even from afar, your love melts me, and with every word, I pour myself out to you.

My Earth! My Mother! I must ask you something—please, tell me the truth. Lately, I've been plagued by dreadful dreams—visions of your suffering. I can no longer keep this from you! In my dreams, all your trees have fallen, and you offer tears at their roots. Sunkhani! I cannot bear this sight; it shatters my heart. My eyes well up, and I weep uncontrollably. There is no one dearer to me than you, my motherland. Please, Mother, without taking me lightly as a daughter or showing any bias, I ask you in whispers, for the pain is too great to speak aloud—could your very existence be in peril?

My dreams grow increasingly disturbing. Even in daylight, I see countless vultures circling above you. The terror of wolves is growing, not just here and there, but everywhere in the world. Oh! Life is so arduous! So challenging!

Dear Sunkhani! What news do you have of your other children? They say that as dusk falls, they wrap themselves in blankets of liquor bottles because they no longer find warmth in your embrace. Your daughters are so frightened that they bury their heads in your bosom at the sight of their own brothers, as if they've seen wild beasts. Didn't you bring them up with the promise of your maternal love?

Oh yes! Recently, someone returning from there told me that when you tried to offer advice, your own son—born from your womb—came at you with a *khukuri*, threatening to kill you. You couldn't even cry openly; you whimpered softly and fled in anguish. Do you understand this, Sunkhani? Do not seek refuge in anyone's home just because they offer fleeting kindness. Do not throw yourself into the trap of comfort and luxury. Do not plunge into the Pacific Ocean seeking coolness, or we will be doomed. Those of us who see our existence only through yours and regard you as our everything will be utterly devastated. I write this with tears as my ink, knowing that my entire world would be submerged in a deluge if that happens. Whether I can rescue you from that immense tide is uncertain! Therefore, before you drown, even if it means playing *Holi* with a couple of fistfuls of blood, I am always ready.

Remember those wicked sons who used to tug at your nose and ears. Out of your motherly love, don't mislead me by hiding them under your arms and saying, "They went that way!" For if you do, you will come to regret it. By the time I have taken that path and vanished from your sight, those wicked sons will have already stabbed your womb and begun drinking your blood.

Sunkhani! Please don't be saddened by my delay. Regardless of the time or circumstances, before dusk falls upon my life, I will bring a handful of white flowers and humbly place them at your feet. In that moment of joy, I will wash your feet with the stream of tears my eyes pour, asking forgiveness for the mistakes I made in ignorance. No matter how heartless you might think I am, I have never forgotten the *Laligurans* blooms of my village, the free flight of the *Danphé*, the cooing of the cuckoo, or the melancholy songs of the nightingale.

I've forgotten nothing because I haven't forgotten myself. ◆

WHY I WRITE POETRY

Roshan Sherchan

When I write poetry, I feel a deep sense of fulfilment that goes beyond words. This joy is more than what language can express; it's an intuitive, lived experience that can't be fully described. There's an aesthetic beauty to this feeling that escapes the physical limits of words, with some part always slipping away when I try to capture it.

In writing poetry, I try to hold onto those fleeting moments that often slip away.

As I write, I imagine a long, illustrious lineage of poets and thinkers unfolding before me. This chain includes figures like Devkota, Rimal, Bhupi, Basu Shashi, Ishwar Ballav, Mohan Koirala, Bairagi Kainla, Shyamal, Bimal Nibha, Govind Bartaman, Manjul, Tirtha Shrestha, and Shrawan Mukarung. It also embraces luminaries like Wordsworth, Coleridge, Shakespeare, Blake, Ginsberg, Lorca, Neruda, and Dhumil, all woven into the same tapestry. Among them, I see countless poets, both known and unknown, whose impact I recognise or have yet to discover.

I see dreams fluttering like butterflies in the eyes of young people stirred by the wounds of poetry. The rich history of poetry fascinates me, as do its vivid imagery and emotional depth. As I travel from the crossroads of history to the present, I find myself trying to carve out a small place in this grand tradition. This effort to create my own niche feels both meaningful and endearing.

Even in its smallest form, I write poetry to see if I can carve out a place of my own.

When I write poetry, I reach back to the annals of history, long before my existence, connecting with moments shaped by poetry itself. Imagination acts as a time machine, taking me to those distant eras when I wasn't yet born, allowing me to witness great poets up close. I look up to them with a mix of humility and curiosity.

I see Wordsworth's Lake District and Tirtha's Fewa Lake as one and the same. I recognise a shared drive in Coleridge and Ballav's search for poetic truth and expanded consciousness, shaped by their interest in marijuana. The fiery language of Ginsberg and Bartaman reveals a common force—one that strips away pretences and burns down falsehoods. The poetic visions of Shyamal and Dhumil unite in their effort to humanise relationships among people. In Shrawan's work, I hear the voice of the marginalised. I am struck by the continuity of poetic essence across different times, places, and contexts. This rare realisation fills me with deep satisfaction, as I see through the eyes of past poets that poetry has given meaning to human life and, in a way, made it more liveable.

I write poetry in the desire to live a little more.

Imagination offers a vast playground, and through poetry, I live more fully. It's not about the length of life but its quality. Poetry provides space for conscious dreams—seen while awake—and filled with vision rather than mere fantasy. Unlike unattainable dreams, those nurtured in poetry have the potential to become reality. Writing poetry has become essential to preserve these dreams, as many have faded outside its realm. It is through poetry that I save these precious dreams.

I write poetry to see if a few human dreams can be saved.

Amid life's temporal constraints, poetry lifts human dreams through the power of imagination. In the monotony of daily routines, poetry adds a fresh fragrance, reminding me that I am alive. I write poetry to protect empathy from fading away. Poetry both burns and chills me—its heat brings the warmth of life, while its chill offers a refreshing coolness.

Sometimes, when I write poetry, I also turn inward and reflect. In the endless flow of time, even after I'm gone, my emotions and thoughts will be preserved in poetry. In its lines, I will remain safe. Poetry becomes a 'mummified' version of my being, protecting my emotions and thoughts from decay. Whether someone will come searching for this 'mummy' in the future is unknown, but those who do will find meanings related to human life within the lines of poetry. It's a beautiful thought to imagine one's soul preserved in poetry for the future.

I write poetry so that I do not die even when I am gone.

The human body has a finite lifespan—it is born and it dies. But the ideas and images in poetry can last long beyond physical existence. Though not immortal, they endure far beyond a single life. Humans have the unique ability to contemplate time before birth and after death, thanks to our capacity of imagination. This is especially true when writing poetry, which is why I write. It is a special experience that I deeply cherish.

This cherished experience drives me to write poetry.

Self-centeredness causes people to shrink within themselves. Living solely for oneself and one's family isn't beautiful, but rather limiting. Poetry frees the poet from these walls of self-centeredness. When poetry and the poet step beyond these confines, they become even more beautiful. Sometimes, poetry lifts the poet to the boundless sky above mountains and hills; other times, it grounds them in the harsh realities of poverty, injustice, and discrimination. In the vast sky, poetry gains expansiveness; on the ground, it gains depth. Is there any sorrow that poetry cannot touch? Even the deepest sorrow is softened by poetry's natural optimism.

I write poetry for the sake of this natural optimism.

I aim to infuse social awareness into the essence of poetry. I want to engage in a dialogue with time and society through a lens of social consciousness. While I understand the challenge of communicating effectively with time and society, I believe we should not let difficulty deter us from this important conversation. Poets are inherently good people, and the essence of poetry is freedom—though not absolute.

There is a unique pleasure in experiencing a moment touched by poetry and then returning to ordinary life, all while preserving that special moment in memory. Such cherished memories become the true wealth of our later years, keeping our lives from becoming bland and old.

I write poetry to keep my life from becoming old.

In reality, there isn't just one reason why I write poetry— there are many. Poetry is a vast womb that gives birth to countless responses. Its scope includes the continuous birth of answers—some clear, others yet to be clarified. Given these many reasons, writing poetry is far more complex than it may seem. After all, poetry is not merely an assortment of letters.

If poetry is the most beautiful experience of the present, it is also the most beautiful memory of the past. That's why I write poetry. So why don't you write poetry too? ◆

ABOUT THE WRITERS

ASHESH MALLA (b. 1954) is a writer, playwright, theatre director, and co-founder and Artistic Director of Sarwanam Theatre Group. A pioneer of street theatre in Nepal, his notable works include the play collections *Anadikram* and *Sadak Dekhi Sadak Samma*, which earned him the esteemed *Sajha Puraskar* in 1984.

AVAYA SHRESTHA (b. 1972) is a dynamic poet known for his subversive, rebellious, and anti-conformist poetry. His notable works include the poetry collections *Phul Binako Sakha*, *Kayakalpa*, and *Lahana Ra Tir*, as well as the story collection *Tesro Kinara*. Shrestha has received several awards and gained immense popularity through his news column *Satyakura*.

BABURAM ACHARYA (1888–1971) was a renowned Nepali historian and literary scholar, celebrated as the 'historian laureate' of Nepal. He is best known for his four-part biography of King Prithvi Narayan Shah and his studies of ancient Nepali inscriptions. Acharya is also credited with the popularisation of the Nepali name *Sagarmatha* for Mount Everest.

BHAIRAV ARYAL (1936-1976) was a notable Nepali writer celebrated for his satirical essays on social, political, and cultural themes. His influential works include the poetry collection *Upaban* and the satirical essay compilations *Jaya Bhuñdi*, *Kaukuti*, *Dus Autar*, and *Galbandi*. He also served as editor for *Gorkhapatra* and literary magazines like *Madhuparka* and *Rachana*.

BHAUPANTHI (b. 1944) is a prominent Nepali writer known for his stories that explore socio-political issues. He wrote under various pen names and published notable works such as *Sambandha*, *Euta Aakar ko Barema*, *Prati Chakrabyuh*, and *Sanakhat ra Aru Kathaharu*. His versatile work spans essays, poems, novels, and dramas, earning him the *Mainali Katha Puraskar* in 1982.

BHIMNIDHI TIWARI (1911–1973) was an eminent Nepali poet, novelist, and playwright known for his social reform-oriented writings. Tiwari authored over 38 works, including poetry, short stories, novels, and plays, with notable titles such as *Silanyas*, *Sahanshila Sushila*, *Samajik Kahani*, and *Bisphot*, which earned him the prestigious *Madan Puraskar* in 1960.

BHUPI SHERCHAN (1936-1989) is one of Nepal's most popular and widely read poets. His collection of forty-two prose poems, *Ghumne Mechmathi Andho Manche*, first published in 1969, received the prestigious *Sajha Puraskar* and has since become one of the most influential and acclaimed collections in Nepali poetry.

BIJAYA MALLA (1925–1999) was a prolific poet, story writer, novelist, and playwright, whose notable works include a poetry collection *Bijaya Mallaka Kavita*, novels such as *Anuradha* and *Kumari Shobha*, plays like *Koi Kina Barbaad Hos*, and story collections like *Pareva ra Kaidi*. In 1970, Malla received the esteemed *Sajha Puraskar* for *Ek Bato Anek Mod*.

BINA THEENG TAMANG (b. 1980) is an educator, writer, and poet from Nepal known for advocating for marginalised groups in her poetry. Her literary works include short story collections *Chhuki* (2013) and *Yambunera* (2020), and the poetry collection *Rato Ghar* (2015), which earned her the *Sulav Tamang Wangmaya Puraskar* in 2016.

BP KOIRALA (1914–1982) was a prominent Nepali politician and literary figure who played a significant role in Nepal's democratic movement. His extensive education and multilingual reading enriched his literary works, which include the story collections *Doshi Chasma* and *Shweta Bhairavi*, and the novels *Sumnima, Teen Ghumti, Narendra Dai,* and *Modiain*.

GOPAL PRASAD RIMAL (1918-1973) was a distinguished poet and playwright who introduced a new era in Nepali literature. Often regarded as the father of vers libre in Nepal, his contributions to prose poetry and drama have garnered immense respect and recognition. His poetry collection *Aama ko Sapana* earned him the prestigious *Madan Puraskar* in 1962.

GURU PRASAD MAINALI (1900–1971) s a celebrated Nepali writer and a pioneer of modern short stories, especially known for his collection *Naso*. His deep insight into Nepali society and rural life is evident in stories like *Paralko Aago, Shaheed,* and *Chhimeki*. Despite a limited body of work, his stories have deeply touched Nepali lives and achieved almost the status of folklore.

HARI BHAKTA KATUWAL (1935-1980) was an Indian-Nepali poet, writer, and lyricist. Known for his unique style, Katuwal's notable works include poems such as *Bhitri Manche Bolna Khojcha, Yo Zindagi Khai Ke Zindagi,* and *Samjhana*. His lyrics were brought to life by renowned Nepali singers like Narayan Gopal, Amber Gurung, and Aruna Lama.

HRIDAYA CHANDRA SINGH PRADHAN (1916–1960) was a notable Nepali writer who focused on social issues. He founded the Nepal Sahitya Parishad and edited several literary magazines. His significant works include the novels *Swasni Manche* and *Ek Chihan,* essay books such as *Junga* and *Tees Rupiyako Note,* and the plays *Gangalal ko Chita* and *Kirtipur ko Yuddhama*.

KUNTA SHARMA (b. 1946) is a Nepali poet and educator celebrated for her satirical critique of gender inequality. With a notable teaching and political career, Sharma is also recognised as the first poet and parliamentarian to recite a poem in the Nepali Parliament. Her significant works include the poetry collections *Ma Ubhiyeko Thau* (1995) and *Mero Manchhe* (2018).

LAXMI PRASAD DEVKOTA (1909-1959) was a renowned Nepali poet, playwright, novelist, and politician. He was honoured with the title *Mahakabi* (Greatest Poet) and is considered one of Nepal's most famous literary figures, with popular works including the best-selling *Muna Madan,* as well as *Sulochana, Kunjini, Bhikhari,* and *Shakuntala*.

MANU BRAJAKI (1942–2018) was a notable modernist and experimental writer renowned for his stories and ghazals that address regional themes and critique societal hypocrisy. His acclaimed works include *Timri Swasni Ra Ma,* which earned him the *Sajha Puraskar* in 1989, and *Annapurnako Bhoj,* for which he received the *Padmashree Sahitya Samman* in 2013.

MIN BAHADUR BISTA (b. 1955) is a celebrated poet known for his insightful satire on social issues and inequalities. His notable works include the influential poetry collection *Sala Pahad Mein Kya Hai*, along with *Min Bahadur Bistaka Kavita*. His exceptional contributions have earned him awards such as *Mahendra Vidya Bhusan* and *Krishna Chandra Regmi Award*.

MOMILA (b. 1967) is a distinguished Nepali poet and writer known for her exploration of patriotism, social justice, and human empathy. Her notable works include the poetry collections *Paiyooñ Phulna Thalepachhi* and *Bhimsen Thapako Suicide Note*, as well as the essay collections *Ishworko Adalatma Outsiderko Bayaan* and *Prashnaharu ta Baki nai Rahanchhan*.

PADMAVATI SINGH (b. 1950) is a renowned Nepali writer and poet. Her first published work was the short story *Patthar ko Hridaya* in Aarati Magazine in 1965. She received the prestigious *Sajha Puraskar* in 2006 for her novel *Samanantar Aakash*. Other notable works include *Maun Akshar, Ek Jhulko Gham, Maun Swikriti*, and *Padmavati Singh ka Pratinidhi Kathaharu*.

PARIJAT (1937–1993) was a celebrated Nepali writer and poet who, despite being paralysed at 26, made a significant impact on Nepali literature. Her novel *Shiris Ko Phool* earned her the *Madan Puraskar*, making her the first woman to receive this honour. Her extensive body of work, including poems, stories, essays, and novels, is celebrated and featured in various academic curricula.

POSHAN PANDEY (1929–1991) was a prominent Nepali poet and storywriter renowned for exploring the psycho-sexual complexities of individuals. His stories, known for their surprise endings and intricate plots, often use everyday incidents and objects to symbolise deeper conflicts. Some of his notable works are *Añkhijhyal, Manas*, and *Hiuñma Pareka Dobharu*.

PRADEEP GYAWALI (b. 1962) is a key Nepali politician and literary figure. Gyawali's literary work includes the novel *Sahayatri*, short stories in *Kuhiro*, and poetry collections such as *Chita Jalirahechha* and *Bina Salik Ka Nayakharu*. He has also authored essays and critiques on political and philosophical issues and has served as editor for various magazines.

PRADEEP NEPAL (b. 1954) is a distinguished Nepali politician and writer. His literary oeuvre includes over 16 novels and 10 short-story collections, reflecting his deep understanding of Nepali life gained through his extensive political career. Some of his notable works are *Deumai ko Kinarma, Ekkaisau Satabdiki Sumnima, Barbarik, Desh ko Khoji*, and *Fewako Suskera*.

RAMESH BIKAL (1932–2008) was an influential Nepali writer known for his progressive and empathetic portrayals of rural life. In 1962, Bikal became the first short story writer to win the *Madan Puraskar* for *Naya Sadakko Geet*. His internationally acclaimed novel *Abiral Bagdachha Indrawati* and other notable works include *Birano Deshma* and *Aja Pheri Arko Tanna Pherincha*.

RAMLAL JOSHI (b. 1979) is a celebrated Nepali writer who received the *Madan Puraskar* in 2016 for his short-story collection *Aina*. He has also been a political activist, journalist, and teacher. Joshi's other notable works include the ghazal collection *Hatkela ma Aakash* (2000), the novel *Sakhi* (2018), and the short-story collection *Ba Aama* (2022).

ROSHAN SHERCHAN (b. 1968) is an acclaimed Nepali essayist, poet, and conservation biologist. His work blends socio-cultural realities with environmental themes, and has published two poetry books and many essay collections, including *Shabdaharuko Desh, Champaran Blues, Dhobighat Express*, and *Galli Sansaar*, which earned the *Uttam Shanti Award* in 2024.

SARASWATI PRATIKSHYA (b. 1981) is an acclaimed writer known for her 2018 novel, *Nathiya*, which explores the lives of the Badi people. The novel received the *Pahichan Puraskar* in 2019. Before *Nathiya*, she published three poetry collections: *Yadhyapi Prashnaharu* (2005), *Bimbaharuko Kathaghara* (2009), and *Bagi Sarangi* (2012). Her latest novel *Swo* was published in 2024.

SARITA TIWARI (b. 1980) is a Nepali poet, writer, and advocate. She has published three books, including *Prashnaharuko Karkhana*, which was shortlisted for the 2015 *Madan Puraskar*. She regularly writes for national newspapers and online portals, with other works including the poetry collections *Buddha ra Lavaharu* (2001) and *Astitwoko Ghoshanapatra* (2011).

SHANKAR LAMICHHANE (1928-1976) was a distinguished Nepali essayist and short story writer, acclaimed for his *Madan Puraskar*-winning collection *Abstract Chintan: Pyaz*. His methaphoric and philosophic essays and stories left a significant mark on Nepali literature. His other notable works include *Gauñthaliko Guñd, Godhuli Sansar*, and *Bimba Pratibimba*.

SHRAWAN MUKARUNG (b. 1968) is a prominent Nepali poet and an influential writer, known for his lyrical songs, drama, and screenplay. His notable works include the poetry collection *Hiu ko Seto Durbar* and the acclaimed *Bishé Nagarchi Ko Bayan*, which has earned him numerous accolades. One of his popular movies as a screenwriter is *Anagarik*.

SUDARSHAN SHRESTHA (b. 1963) is a literary journalist, playwright, and screenwriter, known for his diverse body of work including poems, short stories, and critiques. His notable works include the play *Bhoko Chulho* and the poetry collection *Aago ra Ma* (2018). He has also received numerous awards for his contributions to arts, culture, and literature.

SUDHA TRIPATHI (b. 1957) is a Nepali essayist, poet, professor, and critic known for using satire to address societal issues in her essays. Her notable works include the essay collections *Badal, Dharti ra Asthaharu, Jeevan Sutra ra Swopnabhas, Suit, Tie ra Sungur*, and *Amar Sirjana*. She has also been a professor and rector at Tribhuvan University.

ABOUT THE TRANSLATOR

Jayant Sharma is a writer, editor, and literary translator specialising in Nepali-English translations. He has translated over a dozen notable works, including *Whispers in the Mountain, Rose's Odyssey, Unsung Heroes, In the Battle of Kirtipur, Guerrilla Girl, Gurkha War Poems,* and *Children Stories from Nepal,* among others. As the editor of *Sathi,* a Kathmandu-based English literary magazine, he has actively promoted Nepali literature through translations.

He is also the founder of *translateNepal,* an initiative aimed at bringing Nepali literature to a global audience. Jayant runs the blog *Anuvaad,* dedicated to translating Nepali literary works into English, and is currently working on several important translation volumes. He is also the author of *To Whom It May Concern,* a poetry collection published in Australia.

jayant.catchme@gmail.com

translateNEPAL
literature beyond borders

An initiative of taking Nepali literature to the world.

www.ingramcontent.com/pod-product-compliance
Lightning Source LLC
Chambersburg PA
CBHW051253250626
47155CB00009B/3289